GABRIEL'S FAVORITE HUMAN:

THE ADVENTURES OF ANGELA

A Novel

by JOHN CROFT

Dallas:
Tuckapaw Media

2024

GABRIEL'S FAVORITE HUMAN:
THE ADVENTURES OF ANGELA

Second edition, 2024

Cover art courtesy of Margaret Mercante.

ISBN-13: 978-0-9820698-8-2
ISBN: 0-9820698-8-X

Dallas, Texas: Tuckapaw Media
http://tuckapaw.com

9 780982 069882

TABLE OF CONTENTS

FOREWORD

During Advent of 1997, I introduced the Wesleyan Fellowship Class of Highland Park United Methodist Church to Angela Trufelli in a Christmas story entitled "Gabriel's Smile." The story was written from the perspective of an eight-year-old girl facing disaster by embarrassment. She was to play the Angel Gabriel in her church's midnight Christmas pageant, and everything was going wrong.

Gabriel appeared to Angela to coach her in the pageant role, but she had some difficulty accepting Gabriel, because he was a guy and had no wings—any halfway decent angel would have wings, she thought.

Nine stories ensued. We have followed Angela's life from youth through old age. We have shared her triumphs and tragedies.

The other leading player in this saga is Gabriel. The archangel Gabriel has watched over Angela a very long time. He is her favorite angel, and she is his favorite human.

Each of the following "chapters" started life as a stand-alone thirty-minute Sunday-school lesson. I have tried to collect the stories, abbreviate lengthy chapter introductions, and weave the stories into a unified tale. I leave it to the reader to judge whether this effort has been successful.

This is a work of fiction. If you can credibly claim that Angela was based on your life, I would like to hear your story. If you claim to be Gabriel, the other star of this book, I would be happy to visit with you at my office. But you will have to check in with security first; it's standard procedure.

And now, on to the adventures of Angela.

*Thus ended the foreword
to the first edition of this book.*

It is now 2023 and much, including a global pandemic, has happened since the first edition of the Angela stories was published, Our church temporarily shut down in-person gatherings from March, 2020 to July, 2021, whereupon the class also re-opened. The Wesleyan Fellowship Class asked me to continue composing a yearly advent story and to distribute it each December via email for the duration of the shut-down. I did. Sadly, the class disbanded in late 2022.

I was president of the class during that momentous 2020-2021 era and all the officers tried very hard to hold the class together during the fifteen-month shutdown. Over those fifteen months, I sent dozens of email epistles to the class. Those messages were often informational, some-times inspirational, and frequently just attempts to cheer up isolated classmates.

To go back for a moment to the year 2021, as the Covid-19 pandemic eased up some, Lisa Stewart, the Outreach Director on our church senior staff, asked me if the stories in my "epistles to the Wesleyan Fellowship Class" really happened.

I answered Lisa as best I could: "Some of the stories are true, some are not." A great many of the stories were "real" in the sense that an event did occur. Names may have been changed or disguised. Quirks were exaggerated or minimized; a situation may have been altered or disguised – standard in fiction writing. Every now and then, a story got pretty close to "factual" – like the highway patrolman's pulling over his daughter's high school date when the vehicle refused to shift out of low gear on a major highway. Nice girl, cute too. But there was a bit too much drama in that first (and last) date. Plus, her family moved.

The question about the epistles relates well to these Angela stories. A reader may wonder: "Is this a work of fictional art or a series of personal anecdotes?" I hope you will decide the former and will just absorb Angela and the other characters. Yes, this book is certainly intended to be a work of fiction and classified as a short novel.

Finally, what is new about the book? This edition contains some revisions to first edition language. Times change. There are eight new chapters, the final chapter has been retitled to emphasize both principal characters.

As for Gabriel: I hereby claim him as my guardian angel. Angela made a wise choice.

As for Angela: she is indeed an amalgamation of a few unique and beloved members of the female side of our species. Angela remains consistently human and constantly lovable.

Dedication

This book is dedicated to my late wife, Kay, daughters Karen and Allison, and granddaughters Susannah and Margaret. My daughters and granddaughters may find situations that they recognize here and there in these stories. While I am dedicating the book to the female side of my immediate family, I do not want to neglect my wonderful male descendants, son Michael and Grandsons Collin, Andrew and Jake, all of whom encouraged me directly or indirectly. My son-in-law, Mark Mercante, and daughter-in-law, Ginger Stampley, were very supportive too. Thanks.

Acknowledgements

Specifically, I would like to thank noted Dallas educator Barbara Dorff for her encouragement and constructive criticism. In general, I extend my thanks to everyone who encouraged me to write and then compile the Angela stories. This particularly applies to my friends in the Wesleyan Fellowship Class of Highland Park United Methodist Church, Dallas, Texas.

I am also indebted to Dale and Ted Campbell whose editing made this a more readable compilation. They wielded the blue pencil with skill and grace.

I should also acknowledge the encouragement of the one Hollywood celebrity that I know. Kathryn Crosby, while spending the night with Kay and me before a benefit, stayed up very late reading an early draft of the first edition of the book. She had to get up at four AM for a television appearance, so her courtesy extended above and beyond the call of duty or friendship. She liked the story and encouraged me to continue my writing. Thank you, Kathryn.

Fictional Work

This work is entirely fictional and a product of my imagination. Any resemblance to persons, living or dead, is purely coincidental and unintended. Any errors, omissions, or lapses in timelines or other mistakes are entirely my fault, as well as any typographical miscues. I hope there are very few of those.

And now on to eighteen chapters
in Angela's life.

CHAPTER 1:

GABRIEL'S SMILE

 Angela Trufelli is a bright-eyed golden-haired sprite who had celebrated her eighth birthday last August. She lives in a nice but modest neighborhood in Abington, New York, about a hundred miles north of New York City. Her town is nestled among the hills. Snow comes early and often in Abington and Angela loves the winter setting. Winter means layers and layers of clothes—bright scarves and heavy woolen sweaters. It also means skiing and ice skating and sliding down the icy hill at God's Acre—a nickname for an area in town with no fewer than four churches on four corners.

Angela lives with her mother, Anne, her father, Paul, and Michael, her sixteen-year-old brother—who can be a real pain. Her mother is expecting another child in January. Angela badly wants a baby sister—at least when she is angry with her brother, which is fairly often. However, a baby brother might not be so bad.

The Trufellis were members of the Abington United Methodist Church on Oak Street and had been all of Angela's life. She thought her family had always be-longed there, but she vaguely remembered hearing that her father went to some other kind of church when he was young.

They like the United Methodist Church. It is a beautiful colonial building with a tall steeple. The pas-tor's name was Paul Bonavolante. He had a wonderful background. His father Paul Sr., now dead, had been a second-generation Italian American. Paul Sr. joined the Methodist Church and went into its ministry. His son also became a Methodist minister, but some of the old ways rubbed off on Paul Jr. For one thing, he wears a clerical collar and he likes to be called Pastor Paul. Angela's dad slipped up a few times and called him Father Paul, but not lately. Pastor Paul is a very good man and everyone in Abington loves him. He is the Fire Department Chaplain and proudly carries a firefighter's badge.

This year would be special for Angela at her church because she will play the part of the Angel Gabriel at the annual Christmas Eve pageant. The play starts at 11:00 and ends at midnight with the pealing of the church chimes.

Angela had never been in the pageant before and had never been permitted to stay up that late, as far as she could remember. She would play the part of the Advent angel. Angela secretly suspected that Mrs. Stone had selected her to play the angel because of her name. What could be more perfect—Angela plays the part of an angel.

Now Angela thought she understood Advent. We were waiting for the coming of the Baby Jesus. It was like that at her house, too. Everyone had been expecting, waiting, and preparing for the new baby for a very long time. Angela had heard Pastor Paul describe the event as people waiting for a Messiah, a deliverer. The Baby Jesus would be that deliverer someday—but, of course, he had to grow up first. She liked the part in the church service where the candles were lit—one each Sunday representing hope, love, joy, and faith or was it peace, love, joy and—something. Sometimes she forgot. And she still wasn't exactly sure what Gabriel had to do with Advent.

Angela decided she would ask her Sunday school teacher, Mrs. Stone, the director of the pageant, about Gabriel. It wouldn't hurt to research her character a little bit. Mrs. Stone told Angela that Gabriel was a very important angel—a messenger of God. God sent Gabriel to tell Mary that she was going to have a baby.

The baby would be a special gift of God to the whole world, and Mary was very fortunate to be the mother of such a wonderful child. The child would help the whole world to understand God's love for his people. Angela thought Gabriel was called an archangel because he had a better job than the other angels. Gabriel was chosen by God to do this special work. He was God's right-hand angel.

Messiah was something Angela could understand. That was something like a doctor or Pastor Paul who helped people and sometimes even saved them from sickness or other trouble. She had heard many people say that Pastor Paul had saved them from this problem or that.

Angela worked hard on her part. It wasn't easy. There weren't too many words, but she was nervous to be up on the stage in front of all those people—probably a hundred, maybe a thousand—saying her lines and getting them straight. What if her brother or his friends laughed at her? But her mother and father would look out for her. They would be on the second row, where they always sit when she is in the choir or doing something else up front in church.

A few weeks went by, and the big day arrived: December 24. Christmas Eve was here. Angela got up bright and early and very excited. Angela thought her mother looked very round at the breakfast table. Soon, Angela thought. About three or four weeks and my new baby sister or brother will be here. During a quiet breakfast, everything went a little crazy in Angela's world. Her mother looked over at her father and said, "Oh, my! We're early." Her father jumped up, spilling his 40% bran flakes with 2% milk all over the floor. The dog barked, the cat screeched and clawed Michael, who said something that drew a stern look from his mother. Then she laughed to see her Rock of Gibraltar husband and heir to the family name both go to pieces at the same time. Calmly, she said to Angela, "Well, Angela, looks like the baby decided to arrive a little early. It's time to go."

At first Angela thought, "This is great." Then it dawned on her that her life, as she knew it, was over. The little butterflies in her stomach grew into honest-to-goodness killer butterflies, seen only by the world's greatest explorers in deepest Africa—or maybe New Jersey. In a few minutes she would be alone in the house with her teen-aged brother, whose only interest in the Christmas pageant was Jennifer Cole—who had the role of Mary in the play.

Jennifer was the star. Jennifer was always the star. Worse, she knew she was the star. She was very pretty, but sort of stuck up—like most teenagers. Alone! Alone!

No mother or father to take her to the pageant, to wave at her when she went down the aisle, to tell her after the pageant how well she had done. This was turning into the very worst day of her whole life. She would probably die right there on stage. Mom and Dad would be in the hospital; Michael would be on the front row but wouldn't even notice her death. He would be staring at Jennifer. Well, at least, her brother had entered a new phase in his life.

Last year, Michael would have been sitting in the church balcony with his nerdy friend, Charles. Of course, Angela thought that all of Michael's friends and most, but not quite all, of the boys she knew were certifiable nerds. Charles would probably snicker when she fell down dead on-stage. Alone! Alone in this house with no one to turn to.

Had Angela not been enjoying her tragedy so much, she might have noticed his entry. Although it is still not clear how anyone could have entered the room. Angela had been careful to lock and bolt her bedroom entrance from her nosy brother. Plus, the window was tightly shut. Or was it?

Suddenly Angela noticed someone or something across the room. She had at one time had an imaginary friend named Emma. That was long ago when she was little. Now she was past such things.

Who was this? It surely wasn't Emma. Anyway, it was a guy, not a girl. Whoever it was really dressed as weird as can be. All in white, gleaming from head to foot. With the sun coming in the bedroom window, the figure looked angelic. No wings, Angela noticed, can't be much of an angel.

The figure said in a deep voice, "Don't be afraid. I won't hurt you. I have a message for you."

The gleaming figure asked Angela, "Do you know what a messenger is?"

Angela didn't know what he meant, so she replied "Sure."

He said, "Well a messenger is like an angel, and I know you know what an angel is. I am a messenger and have been sent to tell you that you don't need to worry about your part in tonight's Christmas pageant. You have been chosen to play my part in the play and I have been sent to help you and to tell you that you will be a great Gabriel. You will do just fine.

"You will get to give Mary her great news. I have a wonderful part in the story. It is the greatest gift one could receive—a child. Mary will be so pleased; and you will be the messenger. The baby will be hope for today and for all time to come.

The baby will be remembered forever. He will do wonderful things and help the whole world. And do you know what: as Gabriel, you will be remembered forever, too."

Angela wasn't so sure she wanted to be remembered forever. And how could she play the part of this person in her room, who was a guy not an eight-year-old girl. And he didn't have wings—that she could see, anyway. She thought angels were mostly girls, with wings. As if reading her thoughts, the figure said, "It doesn't matter whether you are male or female. God isn't particular about that in selecting his angels. You will do fine. Trust me."

Angela wanted to believe him, but she was nervous anyway. "Trust me" was what her brother usually said, just before disaster arrived. Her thoughts evaporated when the figure in the room said, "I must go now. Other people need me. There is one more thing, though. When Michael offers to drive you to the pageant, you must accept very nicely."

Angela could not hold it inside her. She burst out laughing and said, "Michael will never, ever offer to drive me anywhere."

The angel looked rather solemn, then smiled and said very kindly, "Oh, but he will. I guarantee it." Then he was gone. Vanished. Disappeared. "Wow!" thought Angela when she had collected herself. What a daydream!

What happened next can only be described as the second Christmas miracle. Her big brother knocked on her door, and after being invited in, as pleasantly as if a human being, said, "Little sister, mom and dad are at the hospital, and you will need a ride to the church tonight. I'll take you to McDonald's and then drive you and Jennifer Cole to the church. Okay?"

Angela thought, "This isn't happening. I don't believe this. I'm still dreaming." But she found herself saying something quite different. She replied, "Thanks, Michael, that's very nice of you. I'd like to go with you and Jennifer." Did I say that? She thought in her mind, as she went to get her sweater, coat, overcoat, and boots, before tackling the very cold weather outside. It was about 10 degrees out there and falling fast.

Things had not gone exactly as expected at the hospital. Angela's mother and father had been at the hospital all day, arriving shortly after nine in the morning. Dr. Schlesinger greeted them and did a brief examination. He was a great doctor and never looked the slightest bit worried. This time, just a brief hint of a furrow crossed his brow.

"Anything wrong?" asked the anxious father-to-be.

"Everything will be fine," Dr. Schlesinger replied, a bit evasively. And everything would be, but in the meantime, there would be some problems.

The Christmas Play was turning out very well. All of Angela's inside butterflies settled down. Michael was wonderful; so was Jennifer. They were into the play a few minutes when Angela checked her watch. It was 11:10—time for her part. It went well.

Later, Mrs. Stone would tell Angela that she had been the best Gabriel the pageant had ever had. "You were inspired," Mrs. Stone would gush. "It was almost as though Gabriel were there telling you how to play the part." Mrs. Hannah Stone had always been very dramatic. She had been a drama teacher at a local junior college before she retired and took up teaching Sunday school and directing Christmas pageants.

The church emptied about 12:20, and people throughout Abington went home from the church—all except Angela, Jennifer, and Michael. In his new role as a decent human being, Michael offered to take Angela and Jennifer to the hospital to see the new baby. His dad had told Michael that the hospital staff would bend a few rules and let the family come see the new baby. Besides, their baby was the only one in the nursery at the time.

They got to the hospital sometime before one AM, Angela wasn't exactly sure when. She had never been out so late in her life. She was so excited about the pageant and getting to see the new baby that she didn't even feel tired; although she knew she should. They came to the nursery first. There lying in a little crib-like bed was her baby—brother. At least the tag was blue. And it said "Baby Boy Trufelli." He was fast asleep and looked like— should she say it?—a little angel. Angela was starting to believe in angels—really believe in them.

A sturdy but very friendly, nurse came up to them. "You can see your mother for just a minute," she said.

When they went into the room, her glowing mother stirred a little, and said, "Hi, angels." Or at least, that's what Angela thought she said.

"Tell me about him, please," begged Angela, "He's so little."

Angela's father answered, "He was born around midnight."

"Yes," said her mother, "that's what the doctor said, although I wouldn't know. Funny, Dr. Schlesinger didn't look like himself, at all. Didn't look like anyone I know. He and the nurses were all gowned in white, and with the bright lights overhead, all of them looked just like Christmas angels. But they couldn't have been. None of them had wings."

"Yes," said Angela thoughtfully, "I understand just what you mean." The others didn't, and they thought Angela had just said a very peculiar thing. They understood the new mom was not quite herself because of the difficult delivery, but why would Angela say something so strange? Probably the late hour. Time for everyone to get some rest.

Angela's father asked Angela if she wanted to know the baby's name. "Sure," said Angela.

"We've decided to name him Joshua," said Angela's mother.

"Yes," said Angela, "I'm not surprised. That's a good name for a Christmas baby."

Now they were convinced that Angela needed to get home and get a good night's sleep. She was saying the strangest things; there had never been a Joshua in the family. The parents just liked the name.

But far away, watching over the little hospital bedside scene, Gabriel—the real Gabriel—wasn't at all surprised by Angela's wisdom and insight. Angela understood Advent and Angela's heart had revealed to her the real meaning of Christmas.

It was almost two in the morning when Angela poured into bed, exhausted but full of the joy and happiness of Christmas. It had been the best day of her life.

Gabriel looked up. He was a little surprised to find that he, too, had been under observation. "Good work, Gabriel," was all the bright figure said, but Gabriel's heart skipped two beats when he saw the smile that accompanied the words.

"Angela Trufelli, you're the best angel ever," thought Gabriel, his face beaming broadly. "You have made me very happy; I have never seen God smile like that before. I just wish the whole world could share such a smile on this Christmas day."

CHAPTER 2

GABRIEL'S ASSISTANT

Angela's golden tresses were flying in the wind as she ran down Oak Street toward her mother, Anne. They were almost late for the Christmas pageant rehearsal at their church. The church was nearby so they would just make it on time. It was a warm day and Angela wasn't burdened by the customary multilayered clothing. In fact, she was lightly dressed, considering that they were well into December.

The snow that usually came early to Abington was unusually late this winter. The hills around town were still sporting scattered leaves on the majestic oak trees. God's Acre looked a little bleak and barren for the season.

The other family member was Charley, a three-year-old spaniel that was especially fond of Angela. Charley was actually a girl dog. Her name had been chosen by Angela as the winner of the family dog-naming lottery. Charley was named after Charles Schultz' famous cartoon character. Never mind that Charlie Brown was a boy. After all, Angela had won the naming lottery, and name the dog she would. Charley had been cute as a puppy with a funny round reddish brown spot in the middle of the top of her head. It started off about the size of a quarter. Now that Charley was grown (and gorgeous in the eyes of Angela) the spot had grown to half-dollar size. Or at least so Angela thought; actually she had never seen a fifty-cent piece. But she knew that they existed, were a little over an inch across, and bore the likeness of a famous young president.

For as long as Angela could remember, her church had held a Christmas pageant. Angela had played the part of the Angel Gabriel in last year's pageant. She was more than a little nervous about this year's event because she had been promoted to Mary. That was a lot of responsibility. Mrs. Stone, the pageant director, had picked Angela because of the great job she had done last year as Gabriel.

Angela decided to ask Mrs. Stone to tell her more about her character. Mrs. Stone was happy to expound. She started off by announcing that Mary was a most important person, the mother of the Christ child. Actually Angela knew that; she could recite the Apostles' Creed by heart.

Not deterred in the least by Angela's somewhat inappropriate reaction to her pronouncement, Mrs. Stone went on. Mary was to have a child who was the special gift of God to the whole world. Mary was fortunate to be the mother of such a wonderful child.

The child would help the whole world to understand God's love for His people. Angela thought being Mary was even better than being Gabriel, even though Gabriel was God's right-hand angel.

Playing the part of a special mother was something that Angela could understand. She would pattern her role on her own mother, Anne Trufelli, who was so loving to her family—plus her mom helped in the education department of the church and was appreciated by all of Angela's friends.

Angela worked hard on her part last year and she would do so again this year. She was just a little too proud of the fact that she was replacing Jennifer Cole as the star of the pageant. Jennifer was Michael's girlfriend and was always the star of everything she did. She was practically perfect—particularly in the eyes of her brother, Michael. As Angela thought about the way Michael carried on over Jennifer, Angela thought she just might get sick to her stomach. Jennifer had outgrown the pageant—and Angela would now be the star—The Star. She will even have her mom and dad in the audience this year to cheer her on. They had been busy at the hospital last year having Joshua, but this year they were hers. She stopped a moment to reflect that Joshua was the best little baby in the whole world.

December 24 arrived on schedule, and it was time for the pageant. Even the weather cooperated. There had been a sudden freeze and a minor snowstorm had blown through—but not much to speak of in this very, very cold section of America.

Angela came on stage promptly at 11 PM. After a few minutes, the new Gabriel told our little Mary her good news—she was to bear God's child. Angela got all of her lines right. In fact, everything went very well. Except, for one slight, minor glitch. During the processional down the aisle, her little girl's instincts overcame her real age. She came to her parents' pew and froze—just froze. Stock still, no control over her voluntary muscles—whatsoever. Her mom smiled and encouraged her on, and the whole thing passed before hardly anyone noticed. The few parents who did notice had to choke back tears, as they thought of their own little Marys—big on the outside, but still so dependent on the inside.

It happened that the proceedings at Abington United Methodist Church did not go altogether unnoticed by higher powers. Gabriel, the real Gabriel, had taken a liking to our little Angela and was watching her. He was very pleased to see how she had grown into the Mary part and was dazzling people with her inner beauty and strength of character. He enjoyed the entire pageant.

Gabriel was, however, horrified as he watched the cars leave from the emptying church. The Trufelli car and a large SUV were approaching each other at right angles on two of the streets of God's Acre—apparently neither seeing the other. The sudden freeze had left black ice on the streets of Abington and the two cars would soon be unable to stop. As the cars came nearer and nearer, Gabriel thought about crying out, "Stop! Stop!" But he was forbidden from directly interfering with earthly happenings.

Then it was too late, neither driver could stop. The vehicles did collide but at a fairly slow speed. After the accident, everyone seemed okay and went on home. But Angela felt a little funny in the head as she went to bed that night. She had slightly bumped her head into the back of the front seat as the car was hit from the side. As she drifted off to sleep, she thought no more about it—

still reveling in the joy of the Christmas story, as told in the pageant.

The next day, her head hurt but good—and she told her mother about her problem. A very frightened mother took her to see Dr. Schlesinger, the family doctor, as quickly as she could. Even though it was Christmas day, the doctor met them at the hospital.

After a thorough check-up, including a bunch of x-rays, Angela was admitted to the hospital—just to be on the safe side. What a way to spend Christmas day.

It was a good thing Dr. Schlesinger was such a careful doctor. Angela started to get worse—much worse. Even though the bump to the head seemed minor, Angela had suffered a serious trauma.

Angela heard the doctor say that she had submarine hematoma, or something like that. What kind of weird disease do I have, she thought? Just before she drifted off into something like sleep, she noticed that Pastor Paul had entered her room.

Later, Angela would remember it as a dream. But somewhere, sometime while she was in and out of consciousness, she met her friend, Gabriel. She was glad to see him again—but a little scared too. He always seemed to be surrounded by a very bright light, and she didn't think he was quite human. She had a hard time accepting him as an angel, for he had no wings. She remembered that from last Christmas.

Gabriel told her he needed an assistant, and she was the best messenger he could think of. She was very pleased to hear him say that. After a while, she noticed someone walking toward Gabriel. He seemed very tall. She had never seen anyone, even her mother, with such a kind face and peaceful composure. She wondered who he was. He seemed much more human than Gabriel.

She overheard him tell Gabriel, "Well, I'll think about it—but you set her up as your helper in the meantime."

Angela went to work as Gabriel's helper with her usual energy. She borrowed some wings on occasion and flew all over the 23 known galaxies (or something like that, as she recalled from an old Superman movie). She helped Gabriel out in all sorts of ways. She was especially good as a messenger to children. Funny, they spoke dozens of languages, but she understood them and they understood her.

She helped young and old, rich, and poor—and she was kind to all God's creatures. She did sometimes miss her family, though—even her brother Michael. Gabriel kept her very busy all the time for what seemed like years. Since heaven time—that must be where I am, she thought—wasn't kept the same as her time, she had no real idea how long she had been in heaven.

But the best thing was—she was being useful as Gabriel's helper. She took messages to him and from him. She helped people, again mostly children, all over the world—and who knows where else—understand the message of the Christ child. Every now and then, she thought it was funny that she hadn't gotten to meet God or for that matter the Christ child. Surely, they must be in heaven.

She only worked with Gabriel, but every now and then she saw the stranger with the kind face talking with Gabriel and looking over at her. The stranger looked vaguely familiar—a little bit like Dr. Schlesinger. But then, not really.

Once the stranger had even spoken to her—she didn't fully understand him (of course). Oh, she knew that he liked her and sometimes silently complimented her work to Gabriel through a gesture or a smile. But one time, he talked to her, really talked to her. He said, "Angela, there are two big holidays in our world, not one; I have no doubt you fully understand the Christmas gift. Perhaps it would be good for you to know more about the Easter gift. I will talk to God about you. You may be able to help people far more than you have ever thought possible." Angela thought—what a strange thing to say to a nine-year-old girl, not even in junior high yet.

Not long thereafter, Gabriel said to Angela, "Angela, I have good news for you. Even though you are the best helper I have ever had, I must give you up to a more important job. You are going back home for a little while—at least the way we count time around here. The way your clock works, you are going back for a very long while."

Gabriel continued, "So as God's messenger, I have a message for you. When you go back to your mother and father and the rest of Abington, remember the man with the kind face. He has arranged for you to have a second chance—of a special kind. He likes you and wants you to help people understand that God has already arranged to give all people a second chance. Now, we don't do this very often, but—you are going back and, in your time, you will find that it is still the day after your pageant—Christmas day. Remember what you learned here—in this short time, you have grown up a lot."

When Angela woke up in the hospital, there was her mother, her father, her older brother and his friend, Charles, Dr. Schlesinger, and Pastor Paul. Dr. Schlesinger turned to Angela's mother and said that her family must have a guardian angel because he had seen two miracles occur in twelve months in the Trufelli family.

Angela wasn't so sure about the guardian angel, but she knew, beyond any doubt, that she had at least one angel looking after her.

Angela thought about telling everyone she met about her wonderful dream while she had been in the hospital. However, she remembered the words spoken in the pageant.

She decided it would be best to ponder these strange and wonderful things in her heart until she got a little older and a little wiser. Maybe she would in time understand why Easter was just as great a holiday as Christmas—but that would take some serious pondering.

And what had Gabriel meant about her having a second chance? Had she been thrown out of heaven? Was she being sent back to do better so that she might earn a place in heaven? Angela didn't think that this was what Gabriel meant.

She had heard Pastor Paul say many times that people don't earn their way into heaven. They get there by God's grace—through a gift already given.

Anyway, Angela was glad she was getting a second chance. She had lots to do with her life. She wanted to make things better for people—just like Mary and the Christ child. As he watched Angela from afar, Gabriel understood everything that she was thinking. And he was enormously pleased. Both Gabriel and the kind-faced stranger smiled at the mere thought of the golden-haired Angela.

CHAPTER 3:

GABRIEL'S HORN:
FRIENDS IN HIGH PLACES

 Angela Trufelli lives with her mother Anne, her father Paul, Michael, her 22-year-old brother, her 6-year-old brother Joshua and Charley, her little cavalier King Charles spaniel. Charley is about eight years old and getting along in years for his breed. The family is planning on getting a puppy shortly after the first of the year to keep Charley company and to make things easier for Angela when Charley goes.

The snow that usually comes early in Abington was right on time this year. The great oaks on the hills around town are sporting majestic winter uniforms The downtown area with a church on each of the four corners of Elm and Oak Streets, known locally as God's Acre, looks like a winter fairyland. What a beautiful setting for a Christmas Pageant—or a Christmas time wedding.

Angela brushes her beautiful blonde hair as she and her mother talk about the wedding planned for next weekend. Angela is very excited because she is to be maid of honor at the wedding of her brother and her friend, Jennifer.

Michael and Jennifer are to be married at five o'clock on Saturday, December 26, at the Abington United Methodist Church. Pastor Paul will, of course, officiate.

The wedding is scheduled two days after the annual Christmas pageant and Angela is a little uncomfortable about not being in the pageant this year. She has participated in the pageant since a little girl. She has played the parts of the Angel Gabriel, Mary the mother of Jesus, and once, a wise man or wise person, as she chose to call her part. More recently, Angela has begun to help the director, Mrs. Stone in many ways. She is turning into a very good assistant director, However, this year, Angela felt there was no way she could participate. She was busy enough with her role in the wedding.

Angela had been surprised, to say the least, when Jennifer asked her to be maid of honor. Angela is much younger than Michael who is 22 and Jennifer, almost 21; but she was elated to be chosen for the honor. Jennifer had always seemed a little aloof, and Angela knew that she had been jealous of Jennifer during Angela's pre-teen years. Jennifer was always the star of everything and more than a little pretentious, mused Angela, somewhat ashamed of herself for thinking such a thought.

Michael just graduated from a Methodist college, way off in Texas somewhere; and Jennifer has another year and a half to go on her degree. After marriage, they plan to go to Cornell for Michael's graduate work.

Angela came back to the present with the insistent ringing of the doorbell. It was Pastor Paul – and he was excited to say the least. "Angela, we have an emergency," he said. A warning bell went off in Angela's head. She and Pastor Paul had a special relationship. She was his utility infielder and had been since she was about six.

If an acolyte got the flu, Angela got the candlestick. She was that reliable; and Angela's mother always felt that Angela was the little girl Pastor Paul and his wife, Debbie, never had.

"What's wrong, Pastor Paul?" Angela asked.

"Mrs. Stone fell off a ladder while decorating the living room of her house. She won't be directing this Christmas pageant, and there are going to be some very disappointed children, not to mention their parents and grandparents," lamented Pastor Paul. The thought occurred to Angela that Pastor Paul must be desperate to be consulting a 14-year-old girl in his time of tragedy.

Then it dawned on her—he wants me to direct the pageant! I can't do that. I don't know how. I don't even know how to be a maid of honor, much less a Christmas pageant director. Can't do it; won't do it.

At that point, Pastor Paul looked her in the eye, and said, "Angela, you are our only hope. The church needs you. Will you direct the pageant on Christmas eve?" The enormity of the responsibility hit her like a Humvee. There were dozens of people in the pageant, mostly kids. It was true that she had worked on the pageant for over five years, including acting as the assistant director for the last couple of years. But being assistant director was a little like being vice president; you sure weren't the commander in chief.

She thought, what can I do to get out of this? But she said, as she had been saying to Pastor Paul all her life, "I will do my best." And now she was into it. Her brother would be furious, her mother beside herself, and Jennifer would faint. Hmmmm, the possibility of Jennifer's fainting cast a different light on the whole matter. Maybe it wouldn't be a total loss, after all. Angela couldn't always control her feelings about Jennifer.

Mrs. Stone sat up in the hospital bed to greet Angela. Mrs. Stone was a ham; there was no other word for it. She made the absolute most of any situation, and enjoyed emoting, whatever the occasion. Mrs. Stone assured Angela that she could handle the role of director, after all Mrs. Stone had trained her personally. Mrs. Stone said she (Mrs. Stone) would probably die of her injuries anyway; so it was just as well to pass the baton to the next generation. Next, thought Angela. I am at least two, if not three, generations removed from Mrs. Stone. It was obvious that Mrs. Stone was in no danger of dying. The hospital wouldn't have permitted visitors otherwise; and Mrs. Stone seemed very strong. But it was also clear that Mrs. Stone wouldn't be directing anything any time soon.

Mrs. Stone said all was in good order; there had been three rehearsals already, and the players knew their lines well. There was only one little problem. Uh, oh! Thought Angela, here it comes. "It seems the trumpet player we hired joined the navy last Monday and is being shipped out tomorrow. We have a nice little orchestra, but no trumpeter," complained Mrs. Stone.

Angela asked, "What's so bad about that? Can't we just leave him out?"

Mrs. Stone was indignant, "Certainly not," she said, "I wrote that part of the music myself. There must be a trumpet when Gabriel announces the newborn babe."

Oh my, thought Angela, Mrs. Stone has broken more than a leg. Gabriel blows his horn all right, but on a very different occasion than the birth of the Christ child. She really has her Bible confused.

Angela had always thought Mrs. Stone to be telepathic, and she didn't disappoint Angela now. "I know very well when Gabriel is supposed to blow his horn, and I can tell you that good directors use their creative talents to the utmost. I have decided," she announced, "that in my show Gabriel will blow his horn to announce the birth of the babe—well a little after the birth, I suppose. I hired a perfectly good trumpeter, and he has deserted me. Now you and Pastor Paul will have to find a replacement. That's it." Then Mrs. Stone lapsed into her favorite role—the good teacher. "You will do an outstanding job—however, we must say 'break a leg' you know. But please don't take me literally," she said extremely amused by the irony in her little joke.

Angela left the hospital and went straight home to be consoled by Charley the spaniel. But Charley was nowhere in sight—deserted me in my hour of need, thought Angela.

The more Angela moped about the coming conflict between the wedding and the pageant, the worse she felt. She needed a miracle, that was sure. How was she going to find a trumpet player?

Far away, overlooking the sad scene was the Angel Gabriel—the real one who had helped Angela once or twice before. Of course, Angela had helped him once or twice also. Gabriel thought, why don't I do this myself? This pageant would have a trumpet like never before.

Gabriel asked God for a short leave of absence to help out Angela. God was sympathetic but told Gabriel he was not to interfere with human history. Just go play the trumpet at the right time and nothing else! "Sure," said Gabriel, "That is all I want to do." God also instructed Gabriel to come up with a believable reason for his presence, and not to reveal who he really was. None of this gleaming white figure stuff. You must fit in with the humans and look like one, too. "OK" said Gabriel, "I can do that."

That very day, Angela went shopping in downtown Abington. To her amazement, there was a street corner Salvation Army band. The little band contained a French horn, a trombone, two drums, and you guessed it, a trumpet.

Angela listened carefully. She thought the trumpet player was really good. "Excuse me," Angela said to the trumpet player, "would you be willing to play the trumpet at our church Christmas pageant? We will pay you."

"I would be honored," replied the musician, "but I won't accept money. I will do it for free."

"Wonderful," exclaimed Angela. "What is your name and how can I reach you?"

"I will just attend your rehearsals, you won't need to reach me," replied the musician. "As for my name, I have a foreign name which is hard to pronounce. Just call me Gabe."

Wow! Said Angela; "I have an Italian name—Angela Trufelli. My first name means angel in English."

"How about that?" replied Gabe.

"You look a little familiar," said Angela. She was too polite to ask him why his uniform was solid white, and all the others wore mostly red.

As if reading her mind, Gabe responded truthfully, "I am new and don't have one of the official uniforms yet. See you tonight at rehearsal."

That night, the rehearsal went much better than expected. Mrs. Stone was right. The trumpet sound created just the right effect. Plus, the trumpeter was really cool.

At least part of her life was going OK—but only part. Jennifer had not taken the news well that Angela would direct the pageant just before her wedding. Actually, Jennifer was the maddest Angela had ever seen her.

"What, you are abandoning me on my big occasion—the most important day of my life. You will be too wrapped up in the pageant and too tired to be my maid of honor. I will just call off the wedding," Jennifer announced. Angela thought this was a bit of an overreaction. She knew brides-to-be could be edgy; but this was going way over the top.

To her eternal amazement, her brother stood up for her. He said, "Jennifer, don't be silly. Angela can direct the pageant with her eyes closed. She will be just fine at the wedding." Needless to say, Pastor Paul, who had been dragged into the issue by Jennifer, was in complete agreement with Michael.

So, there we were—down to the last minute with a nervous fiancée, a harried maid of honor/pageant director, and a completely at-ease bridegroom to be— whose only concern was the rehearsal dinner, and one other minor detail.

Michael had agreed to use some of his high school buddies as the band for the reception. They were the best in Abington, by far. Of course, that was before the band leader, who also played the trumpet, caught the flu, and landed in the hospital.

Christmas Eve arrived on schedule. The pageant was a huge success. After the pageant was over, Angela thanked everyone. She asked the trumpet player if he could stay awhile for a discussion on the music for next year. "Sure," he agreed.

To Gabriel's great surprise, Angela's first words were "Thought you fooled me, didn't you? I knew who you were all along, and I am very grateful to you for saving my life. But there is something else I need you to do. Not only do trumpet players go to sea, but they also sometimes go to the hospital. Seems like the trumpet player for my brother's wedding reception has a serious case of the flu; and he is sitting out Christmas in the local hospital. I need you to play first trumpet and lead the band Saturday night at the wedding reception."

Gabriel said, "This is now Friday morning, and you want me to play the trumpet and lead a dance band tomorrow night?"

"Yes, that is the idea," replied Angela. "I know you can do it," said Angela, borrowing a line from Mrs. Stone.

That wouldn't be changing human history, thought Gabriel; it would be preserving it. Jennifer is already nervous; Michael has now joined her on the edge; and I must do this for my friend.

"Angela, I would like to help you, but I must get permission first," said Gabriel somewhat cautiously. "I will meet you here at the church at 9:00 AM and let you know."

Gabriel closed his eyes and before a star could twinkle, he was petitioning for permission to help Angela one more time. "I am not so sure this is a good thing, Gabriel," God said. It is one thing for you to play a trumpet in a religious pageant and quite another to play at a wedding feast."

"Wedding feast," thought Gabriel, "God can be a bit old fashioned at times." God just smiled at that little bit of irreverence on the part of his right-hand angel.

A wedding is, of course, a spiritual undertaking. Why shouldn't the festivities that follow also be an extension of the celebration? mused God. "You have my permission, Gabriel; but I remind you again, you must not reveal who you are. Everyone must think you are a normal, human musician. But I do expect you to do a good job; after all, you are an archangel."

Promptly at nine, Gabriel, as excited as an archangel is allowed to be, told Angela that he had received an OK from God, but he had to appear incognito.

"Great. Go change clothes; I'll meet you in one hour at Jennifer's house," said Angela.

Jennifer was not pleased with Michael, nor his sister, nor the long-haired, leather-clad musician that Angela had dug up from some rock bar, who called himself "Gabe the Babe." Furthermore, Gabe the Babe announced loudly that he was ready to jam.

"From wherever did you get those clothes and dig that name up from, Gabriel?" asked Angela—getting her tongue and her prepositions all confused. Gabriel was a little hurt by her criticism of his effort to fit in with the music scene. Sometimes humans are very insensitive, thought Gabriel.

"I was told to look the part, and I saw these clothes in one of your newspapers called the National Inquirer, I believe," said Gabriel defensively. "I thought up the name myself."

"It's OK," said Angela, "we can rent you a proper tux without any trouble."

"No," said Gabriel, "I appreciate it, but I have to get my own clothes; no problem."

Jennifer felt better when she next saw Gabe. He looked like the maître d' at The Mansion on Turtle Creek. He was splendid. Angela had him in tow; and they were ready to go practice with Michael's friends.

At the practice session, the other band members were amazed. Never had anyone learned the band's music so fast. He was a terrific musician, by any standard.

The Cole-Trufelli wedding reception went down in Abington history. The band with the unknown trumpeter was totally awesome. He was a combination Jack Benny, Louis Armstrong, rock star, and symphonic first trumpeter. What a night!

After the wedding, Angela told Gabriel that he was her favorite angel in all the world. He told her that she was his favorite human. He added, "When you get around to getting married, just say the word. I will be there with a new trumpet, ready to go. And, when life gets a little rough, as it always does, just remember you have friends in high places. "I can be at your side in nanoseconds," Gabriel said, extremely proud of himself for being so "with it" in the human world.

That night, Angela reflected a bit. God and his angels are right there when you need help, she thought— and up to date, too. At least, one angel is. It seems to me that God always sends his messengers when and where they are most needed.

What a great Christmas!

God greeted Gabriel the next day with a big smile and a cheery, "Well, I see you had a good Christmas this year. You will probably win a Grammy. Who would have thought Gabriel's horn would produce such beautiful, earthly music. Your presence has touched the lives of a great many people; and they are the better for it."

"Well done."

CHAPTER 4

GABRIEL, THE MATCHMAKER

Angela Trufelli lives with her mother Anne, her father Paul, her 9-year-old brother Joshua, and Deuce, her little spaniel who is about 20 in human years. Deuce is Angela's constant companion, sharing all her teenage joys – as well as her occasional tragedies.

The winter wonderland that usually comes early to Abington was late this year The great oaks on the hills around town were bare of leaves and bare of their usual ermine coats. God's Acre, the downtown area with a church on each of the four corners of Elm and Oak Streets looked a little bleak and forlorn. Nevertheless, the physical majesty of the area is inspiring as it always is at Christmas time.

Angela brushed her beautiful blonde hair as she sat staring into the mirror. She was thinking about the annual Christmas pageant at her church which she would be conducting for the fourth straight year—not a minor task for a girl of her age. Angela turned 17 in August and would soon be graduating from high school and leaving for college.

She had made up her mind to go to her brother Michael's college in faraway Texas. Her parents were, to say the least, not overjoyed with this decision. She had outstanding grades and a high SAT score. She was

qualified for one of the Ivy Schools. Her father was forever pushing, however gently, in that direction.

But Angela wanted to be a TV actress and star in
the remake of an old TV show called "Dallas." She had her
eye on the Lucy role. To do that, she should live in Dallas,
she reasoned. All the logic in the world could not shake
Angela once she had made up her mind. Never mind that
the college wasn't actually in the Dallas city limits. That
was a mere detail.

It was a bit of a downer, however, that Michael's
nerdy friend Charles was going to law school in Texas.
Charles Henderson had been a sore spot with Angela as
long as she could remember.

He was seven years older than Angela and a huge
know-it-all. Once he became a lawyer, there would be no
end to his self-proclaimed brilliance.

Angela brought her thoughts back to the present.
Ever since Mrs. Stone's retirement following her accident, Angela had been in charge of her church's annual
Christmas pageant. Mrs. Stone had broken a leg—literally, not just artistically. It helped that Angela had a long
history with the pageant. In her childhood, Angela had
been a favorite performer under the wise guidance of
Mrs. Stone.

Angela paused to reflect a bit on Mrs. Stone—a
first rate ham. There was no other accurate description.
Mrs. Stone was a ham through-in and through-out. She
mushed and gushed and even whined a little, Angela
thought guiltily. But was she effective! Mrs. Stone never
forgot that once she had taught drama at a small

Methodist junior college. Her little munchkin perform-
ers, be they wise persons or shepherds or angels, rose to
stellar performances in the presence of the great Cecil B.
De-Stone.

As she moved into her teens, Angela had been
drafted to serve as assistant director. Then, three years
ago disaster struck—Angela rolled the delicious word,
"disaster" around in her mind and relished the thought
that she too could be suitably dramatic when the occasion required.

Anyway, three years ago, just before Christmas,
Mrs. Stone landed in the hospital—no pun intended,
mused Angela. Angela had hastily assumed the director-
ship even while facing a role as the maid of honor for her
brother's fiancée, Jennifer Cole. Thinking of Jennifer
could lower Angela's spirits in an instant. Not that Angela
disliked Jennifer—it was just that Jennifer was always
the star—of everything. To Angela's surprise and slight
displeasure, Jennifer had turned into a fine wife and was
now the mother of a beautiful baby boy. In her weaker
moments, Angela was sure that Jennifer would name the
boy Jor-El or something suitably Kryptonian. (In spite of,
or perhaps because of, her serious religious leanings, Angela was a big Superman fan.) However, they hadn't. Of
all the names in the book, Michael and Jennifer had chosen to name Angela's nephew after the Angel Gabriel. Angela hadn't thought either of them was particularly religious, but you just never know.

Angela peered down at her dog, Deuce. Deuce had
this wonderful look on her face and was wagging her tail

with twice her usual vigor. Angela knew that this meant that Deuce shared her innermost feelings—or was angling for a biscuit. Either way, that dog had mastered the look of pure love.

Angela was a little weepy at the thought of this pageant—she knew it was her final one at her church, Abington United Methodist Church. She had cast her little brother, Joshua, as the Angel Gabriel—her first starring role. In that role, she had learned that angels don't have to be girls and that they don't necessarily have wings. She had learned that lesson from Gabriel—the real Gabriel. She missed her old friend Gabriel. He had come to her rescue twice and Angela supposed that she would never see him again. She remembered that he had promised to play his trumpet at her wedding, but she wasn't sure that he would and she certainly wasn't in the market for any personal weddings.

Angela wasn't looking forward with much joy to the thought of the big church reunion the Sunday night before the pageant. She had too much to do getting the pageant just right. She heard that everyone was going to be there.

Of course, she very much wanted to see Michael and Jennifer and her little nephew, Gabriel. But there would be others—on the periphery of her life. Jennifer's older brother, Jake and his wife Martha would be there. I think they live in Colorado, Angela said to herself. (In fact, they live in Highland Park, Texas, but have a vacation cabin in Estes Park, Colorado.)

And there would be that self-centered, conceited Charles Henderson—the soon-to-be lawyer. Michael and Charles had given her much grief while she was growing up. She had always wondered why Charles picked on her all the time. It never occurred to her that maybe he liked her and this was just his strange way of showing it. It also annoyed Angela that Charles always described his college as **The University**, as though there was only one in the entire State of Texas.

Rehearsals had gone well. Joshua was a model Gabriel. Angela wondered whether maybe the real Gabriel had secretly helped her little brother with his role. No, she thought. Gabriel would come see her if he were in town.

Able to read thoughts of mere mortals, Gabriel, as he tuned in on the earthly happenings, was greatly amused at Angela's ramblings. He had not helped Joshua, but he would have done so, if needed.

Angela was his favorite human, and he kept close watch over her—all the time. He was in on another secret that would have shocked Angela to the core. For he knew that Charles Henderson was more than faintly interested in our Angela. In fact, Gabriel, was a mite jealous of this human feeling, which he was, of course, not allowed to enjoy—being an archangel and all.

"What are you up to?" The man with the kind face asked Gabriel, as Gabriel continued his earthly observations.

"Nothing," replied Gabriel certain that his little deception would go undetected.

"Well, watch out that you don't meddle with human history, Gabriel," replied the still kindly, but now a bit more stern, spectral being.

"Okay, I know the rules," replied Gabriel.

"Twas the Sunday before Christmas and the entire church was full that night. People from far and near gathered. Pastor Paul was beside himself with excitement. The latest pageant rehearsal had gone well. Mrs. Stone had condescended to attend. She had nothing but praise for her protégé. Again, she gushed that college theatre would never be the same once Angela arrived on the scene—a little chuckle followed her private joke.

Jake Cole and his wife were there from the wilds of Texas and Colorado. Jake was regaling everyone with stories of early mountain men. Angela particularly enjoyed the one about a nineteenth-century English lady who had endured unbelievable hardships to scale some incredible mountains. She had also uncharacteristically gotten herself involved with a dangerously shady mountain man called "Mountain Jim." This tickled Angela's fancy.

Then in walked a young man who took Angela's breath away. Wow! She thought, I wonder who that is? To her amazement, it was Charles the nerd. But he didn't look nerdy, anymore. He looked more like John Wayne than Bill Gates. Nonetheless, she certainly didn't want to give him the satisfaction of catching her staring at him. She was saved. Her brother walked over and cornered his long-time best friend. She moved away, not quite so sure of herself at that point.

From his superior vantage point, Gabriel had, of course, observed all this. With a characteristic, hmmmm, Gabriel thought, I must do something about this—not interfering, you understand, but just helping things along.

In due course, Charles waltzed over to Angela. But he wasn't smug or conceited or brash or any of those things that Angela attached to his character. He merely asked if he could help with the pageant. To her surprise, Angela replied, "Of course. I could use some help."

It is well recorded that tragic things, as well as wonderful things, happen at Christmastime. On the night following the 2006 reunion, Paul Trufelli, Angela's Dad, had a severe heart attack.

It had been coming for years, but the entire family was in denial; and they really couldn't have done much about the situation, anyway. Paul was pretty stubborn when it came to his beliefs and habits. Pastor Paul Bonavolante did his best with the family; and so did their many friends.

Angela just couldn't concentrate on the pageant or anything else. Charles, the law student, volunteered to stand in for Angela as director of the pageant. Since a little boy, he had seen most of them from the first balcony of their church. Mrs. Stone said, "The show must go on." She agreed to help Charles as the assistant director. Now that was really a first—Mrs. Stone in second chair.

Never in his life had Charles Henderson been so worried. He had faked it a few times in class—in procedure or contracts; but he couldn't fake it here. Hundreds of parents, grandparents, and assorted other relatives, and scores of little children, were counting on him. There were wise men, shepherds, angels, Mary, Joseph, and the Baby Jesus—all to be directed and guided. In addition to Angela, Charles was also very fond of Joshua, our 2006 Gabriel.

That night, Charles prayed as hard as he ever had—for Mr. Trufelli, for the pageant, for himself. "Help me," he pleaded. "I don't want to let them down."

This was enough for Gabriel. He applied instantly to God to let him go coach Charles. "He's a good man, God; he has a few faults; but let me work on them."

"All right, Gabriel. You know the rules," replied God.

While Charles was pouring his heart out in his father's den, a bright light from the neighbor's driveway shone right in his eyes. "Good grief, haven't I enough problems without that?" said Charles out loud.

"Please hold it down," said a voice from the now darker room.

"What? Who is there?" said Charles.

"It's me," said Gabriel, no better at grammar than in his earlier visits to Angela.

"Who's me?" replied Charles, "I can't see anyone."

"Let's keep it that way," said the voice, "but I am here to help you with the pageant. I am an experienced instructor in this sort of thing. I helped Angela play Gabriel and Mary. You can tell her that Gabe came by to give you a hand. Now here's what you do."

Two days later—it was pageant time—and Charles rendered one of the finest directorial stints in the history of Abington theatre. Mrs. Stone was really amazed—and that in itself is amazing. She told Angela to stick with acting because Charles just might be the better director. It was a close call.

Not everything in Abington turned out happily ever after that year. Paul Trufelli died on New Year's Eve. Dr. Schlesinger said that there had never been a chance. The coronary infarction was just too much for him or anyone else. But there was a silver lining to that tragic event—Paul endured a minimum of pain and everyone had a chance to say their goodbyes.

Life went on in Abington. The Trufelli family had suffered one of life's major but inevitable events. Everyone who knew Paul Trufelli was saddened but felt that all was well with his soul. He had lived a good life. His memorial service was upbeat. He left a fine legacy.

Charles Henderson was a better man on December 25 than he had been when he arrived in town for the reunion. Angela told him that she would never forget the way he came to her rescue and that he was her hero. She also, not so subtly, reminded Charles that Austin wasn't so very far from Dallas. Interstate 35 connects those cities quite nicely, she noted.

Joshua Trufelli had inherited more than a new family position. He was now the Trufelli star in the annual Christmas pageant. He would move up in Mrs. Stone's esteem.

And Gabriel, perhaps a little somber because of Angela's dad's passing, nevertheless felt that he had once more had a good Christmas. He was morally certain it would be just a matter of time before Charles would tell Angela, "While I was working on the pageant, I had the strangest daydream. There was a bright light and…"

Whereupon Angela would exclaim excitedly, "Charles. You met Gabriel, my guardian angel. That means he must be your guardian angel, too. Perhaps he is meant to be our angel."

At that, Gabriel grinned such an enormous grin that the man with the kind face said, "Gabriel, you've done it again. You are one angel who is not just heard on high—your good works are felt all over God's kingdom. Well done, once more."

Gabriel had one final thought for the day—maybe I will get to blow my trumpet at Angela's wedding—just as I promised a few years ago. Then he took his horn, drew a deep breath, .and out came the most melodious sound one could imagine—"Angels, we have heard on high, sweetly singing o'er the plains." "Gloria…, Gloria…."

CHAPTER 5

GABRIEL TAKES A YEAR OFF

 Angela Trufelli, a sophomore at Southern Methodist University, lives in upstate New York with her mother Anne, and her 11-year-old brother Joshua. Deuce, her little King Charles Cavalier Spaniel who is about 34 in human years, was Angela's constant companion before Angela left home a little more than a year ago to attend college in Texas. Deuce shared all of Angela's joys—as well as her occasional tragedies. The Christmas season is Angela's favorite time of the year, even though she had suffered one of her worst tragedies during this usually happy season: Angela's father died of a heart attack on New Year's Eve two years ago.

Angela is looking forward eagerly to her Christmas vacation from college. She will be leaving Dallas tomorrow for Abington. Abington's usually glistening snow-clad scenery lies fifteen hundred miles northeast from her present location.

Even in Amarillo, it normally doesn't snow this early, mused Angela. Amarillo is a far northern Texas city where it gets much colder than Dallas, but Amarillo doesn't play in the same winter league as upstate New York.

The following day, Angela busily brushed her beautiful blonde hair as she sat staring into the mirror, thinking of her mission project. She realized, a bit guiltily, that she had some mixed feelings about spending so much time at an old folks home at this time of the year. Angela had always been very involved in her church work—but her experience was with children. Specifically, Angela was an expert on children's Christmas pageants. She had played in them, starred in them, and even directed them.

Why should she be so nervous about spending time with a group of senior citizens who probably needed her sunny outlook on life even more than the young kids?

Angela was to finish her visits at the old folks home this very afternoon. The home was called C. C. Young and was supported by her university's Wesley Foundation and other Methodists in her college community.

She wasn't really sure about going there. Angela had a very kind heart and loved just about everyone—but she also felt she had little to say to the residents, some of whom were almost old enough to be her great-grandparents. She knew that some of the "young" residents were born during the Wilson presidency. Wilson was born long ago in the 19th century and had been dead about 100 years, Angela surmised.

[As a matter of fact, Woodrow Wilson was born in 1856 and died in 1924, so Angela's perspective on presidential history was fairly sound.]

As always, she did her duty. Her mother, something of a demographer by hobby, said that Angela would have been a wonderful member of the World War II generation. Angela wasn't sure that was a compliment but thought it probably was.

It wasn't snowing but it was bitterly cold when Angela arrived at the C. C. Young complex for her fourth and final visit for 2008. The friendly staff greeted her and some other college students and took them to a large parlor type room. An enormous Christmas tree stood almost bare in the corner of the large room. There were three or four boxes of decorations with which Angela and her friends were to help decorate the tree.

To Angela's surprise, there was one decoration already on the tree. A single star sat atop the tree. This was all wrong in Angela's mind. She knew that there were treetop star people and treetop angel people. She was definitely an angel person. However, the almost always polite Angela said only that the star looked a little off center to her. None of its five points was pointing straight up toward the ceiling.

That was when Angela met Daisy. Daisy was not a member of the typical old folks corps. She was five feet one, weighed almost a hundred pounds and must have been two hundred years old, thought Angela. Daisy was a familiar figure at C. C. Young. She had survived two husbands, both of whom served in World War II. One had been a General Motors executive and the other had been a high governmental official in the Pentagon. She gave up golf when she could no longer golf her age—somewhere about age 85.

Dr. Lawrence D. Smith, a well-known figure at C. C. Young, was seriously courting Daisy. Daisy referred to

Lawrence as "taken"; but she had no intention of marrying a third husband when her age was in the triple digits and he was ten years her junior. Dr. Smith had been a young surgeon in World War II, a division surgeon during the Korean War, and a brigadier general commander of a hospital during Vietnam.

He always wanted to be known by his middle name, Douglas (named after General MacArthur), but the Army said no; do it our way. It is "last name first, first name next, and middle initial last" around here. Dr. Smith retired from the Army in the late 1970's. Before moving to Dallas, he was chief of surgery in a Canadian hospital.

Daisy glanced up at the treetop and courteously but firmly announced that the star had to go, an angel was necessary. Angela immediately liked Daisy, for she was obviously a soul sister.

Whereupon havoc reigned. The residents divided almost evenly into the star brigade and the angel corps. Everyone was talking at once. Daisy announced that at one hundred and three and with a birthday coming up next month, she was the Senior Resident present. Others disputed her rank, but not her age. For Daisy was indeed almost 104. She had just missed being able to claim a birthright in the far away nineteenth century. She was born in 1905—eight years before Woodrow Wilson became president. Sixteen presidents, starting with Theodore Roosevelt, had come and gone during her life span; and if she made it one more month, she could greet President Obama.

However, presidential politics were totally unimportant right now. The issue was much more important—would the C. C. Young Christmas tree be graced by a star or by an angel. [To those of our readers who think this issue is unimportant to folks with the wisdom and seniority of the residents of C. C. Young, let me ask you. Would you abandon your star for an angel, or your angel for a star? Not likely.]

As Angela was mulling the likely conflict brewing, her thoughts turned to her Christmas plans. Soon the love of her life, Charles Henderson, would be driving up from law school at another university in Texas. She bristled whenever he called his college **The University**, but what could she do?

She had been head over heels in love with Charles since he saved her Christmas pageant the Christmas her father died. But she wasn't so caught up in her *affaire de cœur* to have lost her spunky ways and sense of humor. She would find a way for Charles to enjoy a little humility; it would be good for him, she mused. She and Charles would catch a plane later today and fly to LaGuardia airport and then get on a smaller plane headed for upstate New York. They would arrive around midnight, tired but happy to be home.

Returning to the present, Angela decided that the seniors would have to act their age. She approached Daisy and suggested that the star versus angel issue should be decided a la King Solomon the Wise.

"How might that be, dear?" asked the now suspicious Daisy.

"Well," remembering her Sunday school lessons, Angela exclaimed, "let's cast lots."

"You mean gamble!!" cried one of the more religious church ladies.

Daisy sweetly reminded Church Lady that she knew that Church Lady's primary vacation had been Las Vegas for a good many more years than Church Lady had resided in this wonderful church related retirement home. Church Lady backed down.

About that time Sir Galahad from the law school of **The University** walked into the room. The ladies were much impressed with Charles. He had coal-black hair and in spite of insufficient physical exertion going on in law school, Charles cut an impressive figure of a man of 26. Plus, their young guest was obviously seriously taken with this fledgling barrister. Charles was immediately asked to arbitrate the angel/star issue. Charles, to Angela's dismay, confessed he was a star person but could be neutral under the circumstances.

Charles suggested a sudden death coin toss, and all agreed. Charles flipped his Eisenhower dollar high in the air, and Daisy (being the Senior Captain) called out "tails." Unfortunately for Angela and Daisy, the handsome image of our thirty-fourth president grinned out from the coin lying on the carpet. Everyone agreed that it was heads. Church Lady was thrilled. She had never won anything from Daisy.

With keen disappointment, Angela re-positioned the lopsided star atop the Christmas tree where an angel obviously belonged. This was the first thing that went wrong during Yuletide 2008.

However, Angela was not going to let a minor setback mar her Christmas. After all, she and Charles Henderson would be spending a lot of time together during the holidays in their hometown of Abington. They would go to their home church's Christmas pageant. They would share some of Advent. They might even talk of the future. Angela was quite sure what she wanted in that future, and she thought Charles might see things the same way. [But that discussion was to occur in Austin, not in Abington.]

The second thing that went wrong was that Charles got bumped from their flight. It wasn't entirely his fault, but Charles cut the time a little too close at the DFW airport. He dropped Angela off at curbside and went off looking for cheaper parking. He never found it.

So, he had to park in the expensive parking lot anyway and, after security clearance, got to the check-in counter with about two minutes to spare. The plane was oversold; Charles had lost his seat; and no one agreed to yield a seat to Charles.

Angela went on alone, and Charles followed early the next morning. Things were not going as planned, and Angela's sense of foreboding grew. She had always been a little psychic, her friends thought, although this may have been some of her guardian angel's doing. Angela had the most powerful guardian angel anyone could want—the Archangel Gabriel himself.

Gabriel had come to Angela's rescue on several occasions. She was his favorite human and he was her favorite angel.

From their celestial vantage point, the man with the kind face frequently, and even God occasionally, had turned a blind eye to Gabriel's earthly interventions in behalf of his little Angela.

Now back to Abington: Angela and Charles were feeling a bit more relaxed. Charles had arrived in Abington about two in the afternoon and went to see Angela immediately. That display of affection went a long way toward raising her spirits. For as the song says: little things mean a lot.

Christmas Eve and Christmas Day were two of the happiest days of Angela's life. Charles was charming, witty, and even occasionally displayed some humility— something rare for a senior law student at **The University**. [Angela was, to be candid, a little prejudiced against **The University**.]

Nevertheless, she just knew that the subject of the future would come up in the afterglow of Christmas. And she would just ignore the fact that Charles was somewhat humility-challenged.

Now we come to the third bad thing that happened in Christmastime 2008. Charles' old girlfriend, Linda-Beth, showed up. Linda-Beth's mother was a native of Alabama and insisted that her first child have a proper double name.

Linda-Beth had been cute in high school, but as a college senior, she had moved up to drop-dead gorgeous.

This did not please Angela. Plus, she thought the timing strange. Linda-Beth had gone off to Harvard to study microbiology and had soon deemed Abington to be backwoods and beneath her dignity.

Angela suspected that Linda-Beth had decided that Charles Henderson, the lawyer, would be an acceptable catch for a Harvard woman; whereas Charles Henderson, the former nerd, would not have even made the marriage-qualifying list. Linda-Beth had heard that recent graduates of **The University's** law school were averaging $109,000 per annum—naturally, not as much as Harvard law graduates, but considerably more than BS microbiologists. Yes, indeed Charles had become eligible matrimonial material. Now, all this of course was entirely in Angela's imagination; she had a formidable imagination.

Then, Angela made a youthful tactical mistake. She confronted the poor Charles with her scenario, when the very last thing in his mind was matrimonizing with anybody, even his beloved Angela. He was determined to graduate from law school before even thinking about domestic relations outside of the classroom.

Charles of course, denied he had any interest in Linda-Beth as a lawful spouse, which was certainly true. Rather than stopping at that very convenient point, Charles made the serious mistake of denying that he was interested in tying the knot with anybody at this time in his life. That was not what Angela wanted to hear. She said something curt, stormed out of the room after throwing his Christmas present in the general direction of his nose, and said he could walk back to Dallas for all she cared.

While Angela was enjoying a good cry, Charles went to the nearest sports bar, indelicately named Hooters-Scooters. It may be true that some Harvard women, on average, are more liberated than some SMU women. There at Hooters-Scooters was Linda-Beth, along with about 100 men and one other female sitting in the far corner of the establishment watching a re-run of the 2008 Texas-Oklahoma football game. Charles thought the girl showed excellent taste in sporting events.

Linda-Beth would be happy to listen to Charles' tale of woe. Of course, Charles had better sense than to tell Linda-Beth that Angela was fuming about Linda-Beth, but guess who figured that out in a nanosecond?

Linda-Beth was amazed at her good fortune—but was quite sure she deserved it. Perhaps doubly so, because even "A" students of the male persuasion at **The University**, or any other university, can sometimes be incredibly dumb about women. Linda-Beth led a slightly tipsy Charles back to his home and planted a sympathetic kiss right on his lips, wishing him the best new year he had ever had. Charles was totally taken in—what a nice, thoughtful girl.

The next day, Linda-Beth showed Charles even more of her sympathetic nature by picking him up in her father's brand-new red Ferrari. Linda-Beth's dad was a retired investment banker who dealt in hedge funds, mainly out of the Cayman Islands. Charles wasn't sure just how Linda-Beth's father came by his money, but to his credit, Charles was more than a little suspicious about it.

Charles might be a little naïve in certain aspects of life, but he knew to stay away from potential felons. So it was Linda-Beth's turn to make a major mistake. She hinted that daddy was looking for a good lawyer to help him with his businesses in the Cayman Islands. She even told Charles that daddy's last lawyer quit just when the action got a little too hot. Linda-Beth was really sure that whoever landed her would land daddy's legal business as a package deal.

At this alarming suggestion, Charles put on a very lawyer-like face and asked Linda-Beth to take him back home while he thought about her kind and considerate offer. That wasn't exactly what Linda-Beth had in mind as a deal clincher, but she was very confident that she had her hooks in this boy.

Just after he walked through his front door, Charles called up the travel agent and said he wanted a one-way ticket to Austin, preferably not going through Dallas, and he wanted it tonight. There might be cleverer fellows out there, but Charles recognized a trap when he saw one. Charles felt very badly about Angela, but he didn't care much for her behavior either. He would just go back to law school and concentrate on federal taxes. Maybe he would go to work for the federal prosecutor and put white-collar criminals in the clink. He had one in mind.

But his early departure didn't happen. He couldn't get a flight out until the next morning, and yes it was going through Dallas whether he liked it or not. About nine that night, he heard the worst ruckus at his back screen door he had ever heard. Sure, that it was an animal, he looked around for a gun, but there was none to be found.

Charles' brother had taken the family shotgun and gone off hunting. The Bambis need not fear, thought Charles. His brother couldn't hit the broad side of a barn. Come to think of it, a barn was exactly what his brother was likely to shoot.

Screwing up his courage, he went to the back door with his trusty baseball bat, with which he was rather good. There at the door was Angela, crying her heart out. Her best friend had regaled her with the stories of Charles' being seen riding around town in a red Ferrari with Linda-Beth—sitting pretty close together so the stories went. Of course, two people in a Ferrari will very likely be sitting rather close—by necessity. Angela was more afraid than angry. She made a tearful apology; and to the utter shock of both, Charles also made a tearful apology.

After the emotional make-up, Charles told her he had arranged a flight back to Texas in the morning, going through Dallas, and would she like to come with him. Angela agreed and said that she would like even better to spend the weekend in Austin with a friend whom she had met at a sorority convention. Charles was very pleased with that idea and told Angela that he was quite sure he could arrange for them to sit together all the way to the state capital.

"Charles, were you really interested in that female barracuda?" asked a somewhat offended Angela.

"No," replied Charles, "and I really prefer angels to stars on Christmas trees—if you do."

At this remark, she rewarded Charles with a big Christmas kiss; and Charles thought, well maybe I did learn something this Christmas. Gabriel, Angela's guardian angel, had been watching this entire scene with some anxiety from his heavenly perch. Gabriel laughed and said out loud, "Maybe you did, counselor, maybe you did."

At this point the man with the kind face walked over to Gabriel and asked him if he had been helping out Angela again. "Not this year," responded Gabriel, "but I am thinking about studying up on bar examinations or maybe even proposals; that Henderson boy may need my help more than Angela does."

"He might indeed," agreed the man with the kind face. "I doubt that either Angela or Charles has heard the last of you, Gabriel. Enjoy your new year's celebration; we are going to be very busy this next year."

CHAPTER 6:

GABRIEL'S SONG:
AND THE TRUMPET SHALL SOUND

We resume our story with a flash-back to the beginning of this year—New Year's Day, 2009. Charles Henderson inter-rupted the merry makers at the Four Sea-sons Austin by getting down on one knee and asking Angela to marry him. His fellow law school seniors cheered loudly. Angela, not noted for losing her composure, broke into tears and couldn't say a word. Finally, she managed to say, "Yes, yes," perhaps equivalent to the Spanish *sí! sí!* Which is considered an enthusiastic affirmative, linguistically speaking.

Angela was ready to get on with the ceremony, but they decided the next day that it would be smarter to get married when Angela graduates from SMU in the spring of 2011. Moving along with our story, Charles got his law degree in June of 2009 and went underground to study for the bar. He had already landed the prestigious job of law clerk to Federal Judge Sam A. (Lucky) Lindberg of Dallas. Now all he had to do was pass the bar.

Angela joined Charles for his law school gradua-tion ceremony in Austin. They conduct an unusual grad-uation ceremony at Charles' law school. The Dean pre-sents each graduate with a large sunflower. They call **this** the sunflower ceremony, thought Angela. They must have limited imagination down here in Austin. Instead of donning a hood and wearing an academic gown with three velvet bars on each sleeve, her fledgling lawyer wore a business suit. Her assignment was to fasten the sunflower to his left lapel. **The University** is a strange place, indeed, mused Angela.

Angela spent the summer of 2009 in her hometown of Abington, New York while Charles was preparing for, then taking, the Texas bar exam. She was lonesome and missed Charles greatly. When he surfaced from his lair occasionally and called her on her cellphone, she was genuinely supportive and understanding about his ordeal.

Charles, so he thought, passed his bar exam with flying colors. The results were announced on September 10. He didn't do quite so well on the exam as he had in law school, but he thought an 85 was very respectable. The judge was more interested in the recommendations of Charles' professors and in Charles' standing in his class (actually, near the top) than in Charles' place on the exam list. Charles was sure that there would be some great lawyers, judges, and other leaders to come out of his class. And there were.

This brings us to the present—Christmas time 2009. Charles is busy making his mark in his chosen profession. Angela's decision to stay in Dallas this Christmas caused a general uproar in Abington. Angela had never missed a Christmas at home and she had participated in most of the Christmas pageants at Abington United Methodist Church. Furthermore, there had already been a stir in Angela's home church this past spring. The beloved pastor, Paul Bonavolante, felt a call to change directions.

He wanted to teach homiletics at a seminary. He accepted a teaching job at Perkins School of Theology at Southern Methodist University, Angela's university.

Pastor Paul had nothing to do with Angela's decision to stay in Dallas this Christmas; but inquiring minds doubted—particularly Angela's suspicious mother. Anne Trufelli was sure Pastor Paul abetted this serious desertion. But the simple fact was Angela did not want to leave Charles to the mercy of the court during the holidays. She figured, rightly, that Judge Lindberg would have Charles hard at work in the court's library at midnight on Christmas Eve looking up some obscure point of law.

Angela appreciated that Pastor Paul was close at hand. Paul was very active in the Highland Park United Methodist Church, which adjoins the SMU campus. He persuaded Angela to work in the many activities that the church was preparing for the season.

The church had no real Christmas pageant, but surely that was a misdemeanor not a felony, she rationalized. Angela and Charles attended a beautiful Christmas Eve service at the church. As they strolled from the church to Pastor Paul's condo on Hillcrest Avenue, where Angela was staying for the holidays, they walked past Perkins Chapel. The chapel was a beautiful structure, inside and out. It had undergone a major renovation a few years ago and was the centerpiece of the Perkins quadrangle. Debbie, Pastor Paul's wife, welcomed Angela at the end of their stroll; and Angela asked Debbie what she thought of Perkins Chapel as a wedding site. Debbie and Paul Bonavolante had been married in the Perkins

Chapel in the early 1980s, and Debbie thought it was a wonderful idea.

Angela and Charles discussed the subject at some length and decided they would advance the wedding date a little to next Christmastime. Pastor Paul would work the logistics of getting on the calendar of Perkins Chapel at a very busy time of the year—but Dr. Bonavolante was very good at that sort of thing. He could get a little emotional at times, but he was effective at anything he did.

The Archangel Gabriel observed these happenings from his heavenly perch. He had to remind himself that his little angel was destined to be Angela Henderson in about a year.

Gabriel was somewhat nervous about the whole matter. Would he go to the ceremony in his gleaming white attire, or should he dress in a more muted fashion? Would he and his trumpet be the only music, or would there be other musicians in the service? So many decisions! He remembered well his commitment to Angela that he would play his trumpet at her wedding.

Looking back, Angela and Charles would tell themselves that the rest of 2010 was pretty much a blur. Charles did a great job as Judge Lindberg's law clerk and drafted some interesting and important opinions for the judge. Angela completed her junior year in May of 2010. Angela's summer was mostly devoted to planning the wedding.

Angela reluctantly spent her fall 2010 semester in the "SMU in Spain" program, while Charles continued his clerkship in Dallas. She knew it was the right thing to do for her education; still she didn't want to go off thousands of miles with Charles still slaving away for the judge. She tended to exaggerate Charles' workload.

Her Spanish was excellent but with her long blonde hair, she faced some hurdles in Madrid. She felt that she stuck out like a sore thumb. Charles joined her for a long weekend in the middle of her course.

There are two small Spanish enclaves on the continent of Africa, near the country that was once Spanish Morocco. Ceuta and Melilla are governed by Spain.

On the last day of their idyl, Angela and Charles were walking along a crowded path in one of the enclaves. A foreign tourist approached Charles and asked him in English how much Charles would charge to sell Angela. Angela expected a snort of disgust from Charles and maybe even a fist in the eye of the offending tourist.

Instead, Charles looked at the man thoughtfully and said he would like to think that over. Angela thereupon was about to put her fist in Charles' eye. Charles broke out laughing, and the foreigner beat a hasty retreat. For the rest of the day, Angela fumed at Charles every chance she got, but finally recognized his game and tried hard to forgive him.

Whenever they would have a minor tiff in the future, Charles would tell Angela that he should have sold her in North Africa for the great price she would have indeed been worth. That incident went into her diary, but we are not privileged to see what she wrote. Even Gabriel was afraid to look.

Angela returned to Dallas from Madrid in December to complete the details of her wedding scheduled for Saturday, January 1. Most of the plans had been made that summer and there were very few loose ends. What a way to start the New Year, thought Angela. They planned to honeymoon in Barbados at "Bora Bora," a duplex right on the best part of Saint James Beach. They would occupy the downstairs unit.

A married couple from London had taken the upstairs. Charles had arranged with Hertz to rent a Ford, the only one on the island with air conditioning and automatic shift. Charles would be nervous about driving on the wrong side of the road, but he had no choice. The Bajuns were more British than the Queen. The left side was the right side.

Angela got back to Dallas from Madrid just as SMU was letting out for Christmas. She had strong feelings about not turning into bride-zilla. But there were still a few things to get straight before the wedding. Her mother had been wonderful during the summer planning and was there in Dallas to meet her plane at DFW Airport.

Imagine that, Anne thought: you can get a plane directly from Madrid to Dallas. Angela thought her mother somewhat provincial.

Anne, more or less, thought of Dallas as part of the nineteenth-century frontier. The only city on the North American continent of much note was, of course, New York. New Jersey constituted the near frontier, and Chicago wasn't much better than the western frontier.

California was another world altogether. It was populated by space aliens and their descendants, with an occasional Austrian muscleman—and, of course, their respective followers in the millions. Anne had never forgiven the Dodgers for deserting Ebbets Field for the West Coast.

Angela and Charles attended a candlelight Christmas Eve service at Highland Park Methodist and it put them in just the right mood for Christmas. Angela's mother presided over the Abingtonians visiting in Dallas. Some could not get down to Texas until a day or two before the wedding, but some came for several days. A few stayed at the Gaylord Texas and certainly got an eyeful of one establishment's idea of what Texas was all about. A few opted for the Anatole, and the rest stayed at a half dozen other hotels around the city.

Angela had delegated one item to Pastor Paul. She and her mother were simply too busy for her to arrange the music for the wedding. She knew Pastor Paul had conducted hundreds of weddings, including several in Dallas. There was no doubt in her mind that he could find an organist and a trumpet player as well.

Shortly before the wedding, Pastor Paul told Angela that he had found just the right trumpet player to accompany the Highland Park Church organist. In fact, it was like a godsend because a trumpet player had come to Pastor Paul a few days before, looking for a job. Upon hearing him once, Pastor Paul signed him up immediately.

Paul thought to himself that it was a little funny that the musician's name was Gabriel di Angelo. There are lots of coincidences in this world; this is just one more. Pastor Paul had decided to spare Angela the details. She had enough on her mind.

Somewhat more worrisome, Gabriel had come back the next day to see pastor Paul. After some hedging, Gabriel said, "Let's use English in the pronunciation of my name. Almost nobody calls me Gabriel—it's Gabe, pure and simple. Ummm, what I want to talk with you about is a little delicate. I would urge you to get a backup chapel for Angela's wedding ceremony. I have a bad feeling about the location, the weather and all."

As you will recall, Gabriel was forbidden to change human history; but he knew that on January 1, Dallas would face the worst freeze in over 50 years. He also knew that on that day Perkins Chapel would be without electricity but that the nearby Highland Park Church would weather the storm. Gabriel, however, couldn't tell Dr. Bonavolante what was going to happen without violating his instructions.

All he could do was try to get Pastor Paul to set up a contingency plan—which, of course, had never been done before. Fortunately, Dr. Bonavolante and Dr. Marco Vincenzo Peel, the church's senior pastor, were the best of friends. Over the years, Dr. Peel had suffered some razzing because of the similarity of his name with that of a very famous New York preacher.

Dr. Peel was quick to point out that his last name was spelled P-E-E-L, as in Sir Robert of Scotland Yard.

Besides his first and middle names were Italian. Marco was fourth generation half-Italian and sympathetic to Pastor Paul, a compatriot. Pastor Paul was still a bit nervous about this arrangement. Cox Chapel was to take on a new role in the contingency set-up. Marco signed on to the deal—good thing, too.

On December 31, the storm hit. That night, it was colder in Dallas than in upstate New York where Angela and Charles had spent most of their young lives. Abington recorded a low of 15 degrees F. on December 31, and Dallas enjoyed a record low of 10 degrees below zero.

In Dallas, the wedding day warmed up considerably. The temperature was just under 30 degrees F. at 4 o'clock that afternoon. Angela and her mother took the event in stride and were very impressed that Pastor Paul could move the service from Perkins to Highland Park's Cox Chapel on such short notice.

They thought Pastor Paul a miracle worker. Hmmmm, thought Gabriel, with a note of slight jealousy, unusual for an archangel.

On the wedding day, Angela had only one meltdown or temper tantrum or bride-zilla occurrence, as she called it. The photographer thought his assistant had the extra memory card and the assistant thought the photographer had it. Angela, to her credit, calmed down after a bit. The assistant simply had to find a proper memory card, and she did so in less than an hour. The fact that it was New Year's Day, with most stores closed after the huge storm had passed, was a mere trifle.

It seemed to Charles that his beautiful bride-to-be was showing considerable fang. However, he was also well aware that he had only one duty—to show up. He was not there to make decisions or help or anything else; he was there to be there.

Six o'clock in the evening arrived and everyone was in his or her place. Pastor Paul knew the ropes and kept a calming hand on the groom and his attendants.

Angela was to be given away by her mother. Michael, Angela's older brother, was to accompany Angela down the aisle. Angela had planned this arrangement since her father's death four years earlier.

Michael was pleased to be selected for this honor and almost broke down when *The Prince of Wales March* began and it was time to escort his little sister down the aisle to meet his best friend, Charles. "Don't lose it, old boy," Michael said to himself.

Then the most glorious trumpet sound Michael had ever heard joined the organ in playing *The Prince of Wales March*, and Michael almost lost control after all. Angela, not easily surprised, gave a visible start and desperately wanted to look back and up into the chapel balcony to see who was playing the trumpet.

However, in her heart, she knew who it was. There was only one being in the universe who could play like that. It had slipped her mind that Gabriel had promised to play at her wedding. Reaching the right conclusion in a moment, she beamed her dazzling smile—at Charles in the front of Cox Chapel, not at Gabriel in the back of the balcony.

But Gabriel could read human thoughts, and he was very pleased with himself. The ceremony was beautiful, and Gabriel did the recessional with his usual aplomb. Everything was perfect.

Pastor Paul had noticed more than Gabriel was comfortable with and had asked Gabriel to stay after the wedding reception because he had a few questions for him. However, Gabriel unfortunately had to leave near the end of the reception, mumbling something about having to fly off somewhere.

Our couple traded the cold weather in Dallas for a warm beachfront duplex in Barbados. The older couple upstairs, in their forties, made the newlyweds feel very welcome. Next year, the old timers would rack up fifteen consecutive years at Bora Bora

Charles had no serious driving problems, but Angela was nervous that he would drive into the deep ditch by the left side of the road. Barbados had no roadside curbs except in Bridgetown, the capital city.

Once, they drove out to the Atlantic side of the island to a place called Sam Lord's Castle. It really looked like a castle and Angela thought it looked spooky. The Atlantic Ocean is much rougher than the Caribbean Sea, and there were signs everywhere warning the tourists not to swim in the Atlantic. The natives didn't need a sign, they knew better than to enter the ocean in January.

A week passed, and it was time to abandon Eden for the real world. Charles had to return to Dallas to keep his judge out of hot water, and Angela had to finish her final semester at SMU. They rented a nice condo near

Pastor Paul's home. The location was ideal for Angela and convenient for Charles.

That spring, Hexi-All Corporation, the world's largest energy company offered Charles a job in its law department in New York City. True, with his grades and the federal clerkship behind him, Charles could have joined a "white shoe" law firm and sooner or later enjoyed a lucrative partnership in private practice. His new employer, Hexi-All, drew its name from the fact that it had petroleum operations on six continents.

However, he was intrigued by the prospect of joining an organization with 500 lawyers and operations in 100 countries. He told Angela that he was choosing adventure over riches. He also promised Angela that if she stuck with him, she would never be bored. Looking back some years later, she told Charles that his promise had turned out to be accurate.

Angela and Charles would almost be moving back home. Charles would commute to the city from their new home in New Canaan, Connecticut. They felt this was a great way and a great place to begin their new life together. The town's slogan was "next stop to heaven." Angela thought it was a clever joke. But it turned out, as we shall see, that the locals were dead serious about their motto.

Charles and Angela had some of the usual trials and tribulations of newlyweds in a strange new land; but as Gabriel was fond of saying, "This couple is right for each other, and I know that they won't find their life boring. Besides, I will keep an eye out on them—just to make sure."

CHAPTER 7

ANGELA REFLECTS
ON HER HALCYON DAYS

 As she lounged on her daybed in her lovely New Canaan home, Angela in her thoughts, turned back the pages of time to the holiday season of 2010.

She and Charles Henderson have just been married in Cox Chapel of Highland Park United Methodist Church in the beautiful Dallas suburban enclave of Highland Park. They were united in marriage by their old family friend, Pastor Paul Bonavolante. Angela and Charles had planned to marry in Perkins Chapel on the Campus of Southern Methodist University, but the venue was changed because a severe storm disrupted the electricity in Perkins Chapel, sparing Cox Chapel, however.

Angela asked Pastor Paul to arrange for the music. He recruited a marvelous trumpet player to accompany the greatly talented organist at Highland Park. The trumpeter turned out to be none other than the Archangel Gabriel in disguise. Only Angela recognized her old friend and personal guardian angel.

As she continued her reverie, she thought about their honeymoon on the island of Barbados in a duplex beach house named "Bora Bora" on St. James Beach. They loved their week in Barbados, in spite of having to drive on the wrong side of the road, the time to return to Dallas arrived quickly. They had some important unfinished business. Angela needed to graduate from SMU, and Charles needed to finish his clerking assignment for Federal Judge "Lucky" Lindberg.

In the Spring of 2011, Charles accepted a job in the New York Law Department of Hexi-All Corporation, the world's largest energy company. Hexi-All had over 500 lawyers in 100 countries around the world. Both Charles and Angela saw this opportunity as the great adventure that it indeed turned out to be Charles frequently told Angela that he had chosen adventure over riches and that she would never be rich or bored. In retrospect, she would have to agree that boredom seldom entered her life. As for adventure instead of riches: Well, Charles did okay in the compensation department, too.

As Angela thought about their extremely happy days of early marriage, Angela and Charles decided to live in a lovely New York outer suburb in next door Connecticut. Charles' boss lived there and had encouraged Charles to do so too. It was a stretch of their finances, but the public schools were top notch: and that helped the overall budget – no need for a private school. Also, the newcomers club was every active, and that was a help to Angela. Angela had such a bright personality that she didn't need too much help, but friendly neighbors are always a blessing.

One of those neighbors was Emily Fuddrucker. Emily was president of the New Canaan Newcomers Club and always held the first dinner party of the year. Angela had just joined the club and had some reservations about Emily, as well she might. The first party was scheduled for the third Friday in October. Angela and Charles were pretty astute for being so young. They checked out the scene. One thing they discovered was hard to believe. It seems that if a party were scheduled for 7:30 anyone who arrived before eight was considered rude as well as early. This was a universal rule for almost all New Canaan functions. So, Charles dubbed the late social hours as "New Canaan Rules." This was somewhat like the "Moscow Rules" in the LeCarre novels. In other words, it didn't matter what the words said, you knew what you were supposed to do – arrive 30 minutes after the appointed hour.

So, Charles and Angela dutifully arrived at 8 for their first newcomers' dinner at Emily's house. The first unusual thing that happened was the Emily made everyone put their coats on the guest bed, even though the hall closet was empty.

The next unusual thing was that after the appetizer, Emily had a coughing fit and accused her husband of neglecting to use the Heimlich maneuver, intending that she choke to death. About that time, three couples remembered they had to rush home to check on their new babysitter, since she was a first timer and they were scared she didn't know what she was doing. Several other couples admired the three couples' ingenuity and wished they had been that clever.

It didn't bother Charles when the conversation got around to the latest oil shortage. Some of the guests were hostile to the petroleum industry certain that there was a conspiracy with tankers out there just beyond the twelve-mile limit loaded with oil. Charles was, however, a little surprised when one of the New Canaanites blamed daylight savings time on an oil industry plot to sell more gasoline.

The final unusual thing happened right after dessert. Angela went into the kitchen and offered to help wash the dishes. Emily graciously declined and continued counting something. Angela asked her what she was doing.

"Counting the silver, of course," said Emily. "Silver is very expensive, and guests steal the silverware all the time."

At that point, Angela rushed into the den interrupting Charles' lengthy explanation of some obscure but important legal point to a local investment banker's drop-dead gorgeous trophy wife who was hanging on to every word Charles had to say.

Charles thought he was in big trouble, but Angela was not mad about the somewhat overlong legal explanation. She was just intent on leaving the party before Emily planted some hot silverware in their overcoats. She vaguely remembered the biblical story of Joseph's planting some contraband in his brothers' carryon luggage. It was a strange evening.

Angela found herself with some morning discomfort in their third year in New Canaan. She was 99 44/100 per cent sure she was pregnant and was nervous at the thought that Charles was hours away at best and at the mercy of the New Haven Line. Nevertheless, like millions of others, they braved her first pregnancy quite well.

Charles had recently assumed a great training assignment as assistant to the president, and the president told him no one on the 51st floor had ever produced a baby before while working at such a lofty level. But then, no thirty-year old had ever officed on the 51st floor, either. The other suits were at a loss as to how to handle the situation. So, they just pretended that there were no baby makers at that altitude. Charles was greatly amused but knew better than to overplay his hand. The 51st floor was a land of great opportunity but it could be a place of real peril if you messed up.

In due course, baby Margaret appeared. Everyone was duly impressed. She weighed in at 7 pounds and 10 ounces and measured 20 inches. Angela and Charles were very proud parents of this their first of three offspring.

"Oh my. I am really drifting away into dreamland," Angles said to herself as she stirred back into the real world. Charles will be home at any moment, and I've done nothing about dinner. Looks like a good night to wander over to Westport and eat at Pancho's, a self-proclaimed Tex-Mex restaurant. Pancho's was a popular spot because it was rumored that two local celebrities dined there often, but Angela had never spotted hide nor hair of either Butch Cassidy or his lovely wife.

About then Charles arrived and Angela said: "Let's do Westport tonight, I have a yen for Mexican."

Charles replied, "Sure but I think it's "ole Blue Eyes" you're hoping to run into."

Angela responded in timely fashion with, "Not so: why should I, when I have young Blue Eyes. Let's grab the kids and head East."

CHAPTER 8

ANGELA'S SOUTH AMERICAN ADVENTURE

 It was a dreary mid-December day in New Canaan, Connecticut. In fact, it was cold as well as raining cats and dogs. Angela Henderson was at her computer working on her annual Christmas Pageant for The New Canaan United Methodist Church. She was annoyed at her husband Charles. Charles had called her from his office in New York City about three hours ago and told her to standby for some great news he would be home soon with those glad tidings but she was nervous that it meant a new assignment for Charles in that great conglomerate, Hexi-All Corporation.

Charles reported directly to the President of the corporation and enjoyed a very good relationship with the big boss. Angela loved New Canaan and had no reason to want to uproot to some remote location, like Midland, Texas or Baton Rouge, Louisiana or heaven forbid, Billings, Montana, all offering a tremendous opportunity for advancement of course. Angela thought that they had already advanced well up the pay scale. On the other hand, she did not want to dampen Charles enthusiasm for whatever might be their fate.

Charles bounded into the family room about that time and announced: "I have great news: we have been selected to go to Bogota for a short training assignment. I will be the acting marketing Vice President and responsible for six countries, in which we have a 40% market share. Isn't that great?"

Angela had a somewhat different view of things. It was almost Christmas, plus she didn't think the Bogota that Charles was referring to was the somewhat questionably pronounced Bo-**Go**-Ta in Texas near her Alma Mater, Southern Methodist University. It was likely the one in Colombia, South America—land of famous drug lords, offering the excitement of a few random murders.

"Charles, I think this may be wonderful for your career, but I just don't see how I can work it into my schedule," responded Angela a bit too fast on the draw.

Then she had an afterthought. "Charles, is that the South American affiliate with the female general counsel we met last summer at the New Trade Center Club?" subtly asked Angela.

"Yes, I think it is," answered Charles.

Angela continued. "You know, the woman lawyer named Señora Pilar Santana de López y García—the one with the skintight dress, slit up to *here*, who insisted on doing the tango with you on the tiny dance floor?"

"Well, I believe that is the one," replied Charles.

"Give me thirty minutes to finish writing my Christmas pageant and fifteen minutes to call the doggie hotel for Charley III (their Cavalier King Charles Spaniel) and fifteen more to pack my bags; for our trip to beautiful Bogota," said Angela with genuine excitement in her voice. Actually, it took a bit longer.

Angela has vivid memories of the female barracuda from Harvard who almost stole Charles when the couple suffered a minor premarital difference of opinion. The Harvard teeny bopper wasn't even on the same planet as Señora Pilar Santana de López y García.

Dr. Williams, the president of Hexi-All had almost swallowed his dental implants when Pilar clamped a rose in her mouth and showed Charles the latest Colombian tango steps That was just before the club DJ asked Charles to do a Tahitian grass skirted fertility dance with a professional dancer named Omi-Omi.

Pilar was very miffed at the DJ, since she expected Charles' sole attention in that cozy space. At that point, Dr. Williams intervened and wisely left the dance arena with Charles in tow so they could discuss important company business in the executive washroom. To be honest, Charles was grateful because he wasn't at all sure he was up to a Tahitian fertility dance with a grass skirted alleged Tahitian maiden.

Later Charles had discussion with his good friend, Chauncey Dewey Butterworth IV, BA (Yale), MBA (Harvard), junior partner in his father's hedge fund management company, about the DJ and Omi-Omi. Chauncey assured Charles that he, Chauncey Dewey Butterworth IV, had it on good authority that Omi-Omi was definitely not a Tahitian maiden. It was not clear to Charles whether the denial related to the word Tahitian or the word maiden or both. Chauncey did say that Omi-Omi was very talented and could shake a mean grass skirt – when inspired. Charles left it at that, discretion being the better part of valor.

On Wednesday next at 8AM EST, Charles and Angela boarded Avianca Aerolíneas SA, flight 007 nonstop from JFK airport to Bogota. The flight took just under six hours. There were eight other seats in the first-class compartment. And Charles thought all eight were occupied by tough looking hombres (that's Spanish for banditos) or their female companions. One of them asked Charles where he (Charles) was staying, and Charles reluctantly told him the Hotel Europa Grande. Charles' new friend, Juanito, the really tough looking one, said. "Mind if my *esposa* [that's Spanish for significant other of the female persuasion] and I share a taxi with you and your *esposa*? We are staying at The Hotel Europa Grande, too."

Charles decided this was an offer he shouldn't refuse. So Charles said something to the effect of "*Mais Oui.*" [which is French for "Sure"] Wrong language, you Dummy, Charles said to himself.) Charles recovered with a "*Sí, Sí, Señor.*"

After a few days in the Hotel Europa Grande, Charles and Angela moved into a swanky gated community that housed the former Vice President for Marketing of Hexi-All Colombiana SA and a number of other senior executives of major American owned corporations. It came with a housekeeper, Maria, and her husband, Jorge Simon Carlos Washington Bolivar. The first in-house assistant was called Maria and was a treasure.

Her husband, the second in-house assistant, went by the name of Carlito. Charles could not help noticing that there was a sizable bulge in the front of the left side of Carlito's expensive silk jacket, Charles decided not to comment on the ill-fitting suit, but did observe that Carlito was right-handed. Carlito turned out to be a quick get-away artist, but Charles declined to comment on that idiosyncrasy as well.

The President of Hexi-All Colombiana took Charles and Angela by the US Embassy at the first opportunity and introduced them to a number of key officials including the First Secretary. The First Secretary had to rush off to meet a visiting dignitary at the Bogota airport, so the First Secretary passed them to the Second Secretary who turned out to be a delightful woman a little older than Angela.

The Second Secretary was a Georgetown University graduate of some ten years past and relatively new to Colombia She had been posted to Buenos Aires for almost five years as Third Secretary and was fluent in Spanish. In fact, she graduated from the Walsh School of Foreign Service at Georgetown fluent in Spanish.

The Colombians claimed they spoke the purest Spanish on the Globe, far superior to the language spoken in the Mother Country, *España* – even the Castilians. The delightful lady introduced herself as Eleanor Squibb Merck, and said she would be honored to show Angela some of the sights of Bogota and surrounding areas.

Charles thought this was the answer to his prayers. Angela would escape the usual boredom of the corporate wife who was tagging along on a special assignment Also, she would be in the protective custody of an American diplomat with that precious diplomatic license plate. Surely no violence could befall his beloved Angela in such circumstances. Plus, he suspected anyone with the middle and last names of Squibb and Merck was likely able to hold her own in the pricey shops of Bogota.

One thing Charles didn't put into the equation, however, was that there was a criminal element who would be very attracted to the funds likely available to ransom someone named Eleanor Squibb Merck and the wife of a senior executive of Hexi-All Corporation. [It should be noted that Charles would never be this naïve again.] Of course, Carlito thought it was his job to protect Angela, with his very life – just as the Embassy security team felt obliged to protect Eleanor.

The Embassy Head of Security, Adolf Kreuger looked every bit as tough as Carlito and amply able to carry out his responsibilities. It might be noted that there was some good natured, most of the time, rivalry between Carlito, who was probably on the Hexi-All security payroll, and Adolf, who was definitely on the US Embassy payroll—although somewhat obliquely.

Let us for a moment go back to Charles' first-class compadres and taxi-ride sharer, Juanito. Juanito and his compadres were very interested in their new American friend Charles. Juanito said something to the effect that: He would like to get to know the idiot gringo (seems Juanito comes from Mexico) a whole lot better. He looked like an easy mark, or words to that effect, Diego, Manuel and Pablo quickly agreed with Juanito, as they always did. Not to agree with Juanito was usually associated with harsh painful memories. Yes, Juanito was a mid-level Jefe in one of the Colombian gangs. It's hard to keep them straight, but he was definitely not a drug lord.

Angela called up her new friend Eleanor at the Embassy and said she wanted to go see the *Valle de Cocora*, which is located about halfway between Bogota and the Pacific Ocean, and would Eleanor go with her. Eleanor thought sightseeing in the *Valle de Cocora* was a great idea. Eleanor told Angela she would love to go and would have the Embassy secure the park tickets and make the travel arrangements.

The *Valle de Cocora* is a protected area in Quindio near the eco-tourist/backpacker haven Salento. "It has a striking landscape pegged with the slender towering Colombian national symbol, the Wax Palm." read Angela, paraphrasing the tourist guide. The trees were no longer endangered but the area had been designated a protected park in the nick of time to save the trees. The park is one of the few places in the world where you can find these immense trees.

The American Embassy arranged air travel for Angela and Eleanor from Bogota to Pereira, about an hour's flight. The Embassy also arranged for a car and driver to take them from the Pereira Airport to their hotel in Salento, the jumping off place for coffee farm, the Los Nevados National Park and best of all, the Valle de Cocora. Adolph, the Embassy security chief, assigned Jose to meet the ladies at the airport and to be their driver for the duration of the trip. José had been a member of the Embassy security team for about ten months. However,

Adolph wasn't convinced of José's skills in personal protection.

José was a skilled driver though and had consistently performed that part of his assignment well, but his English was rather poor. Eleanor would be there to translate, so, Angela felt very secure.

The next morning, José picked the ladies up at the Salento Hotel and dropped them off at the park entrance. José told Eleanor that he would meet them at the snack bar in 30 minutes. He had to get some petrol for the car. Angela thought that a little unusual, why hadn't José filled up in Salento? But Eleanor didn't seem concerned at all.

What none of them knew was that Carlito had taken an earlier flight and was already in the park and fully on guard to watch over Angela.

Also watching Angela and Eleanor arrive at the park were Diego, Manuel, Pablo and a local bandito nicknamed "Cabrito." Now the *Little Goat* may seem to be a strange name for a gangster, but there was nothing little about Cabrito.

Nor was there anything small about the Glock 9mm he kept tucked under his shirt. Diego asked Cabrito where their man Jose was in all this, Cabrito just said, "We can trust Jose. He's set these two *chicas* up for us to grab when they are alone out in the park."

Diego was a little nervous about the entire situation, Juanito didn't often trust his underlings to carry off any job without his personal supervision, but Juanito was in Bogota at a meeting with a big jefe. Diego was in charge of the kidnap job. It should be a snap, since the ladies' security was in their pocket.

But there were a couple of things the gangsters didn't know. The first thing was that Carlito was a very well-trained security operative who also carried a Glock 9mm automatic in his shoulder holster.

The other thing they didn't know was that Eleanor was not exactly what she seemed. Eleanor had undergone Seal training in the Navy and graduated at the top of her class. She was also *not incidentally* an experienced CIA agent. Eleanor manned a Baretta and was just as deadly as Carlito. The four banditos were very likely out of their league in the *Deadly* department.

Neither Eleanor nor Carlito was particularly adept in the due process department. But who's perfect?

Eleanor had mapped out a plan for their hike. They would hike through the valley, into the woods up through the cloud forest, to the Hummingbird Farm, then turn around and finish hiking up the mountain and ending at the main attraction – The Wax Palm Trees.

When Jose didn't show up at the appointed time Eleanor and Angela went ahead and had their snack and decided to head off up the trail, Jose knew their plan and he could just catch up with them. Jose was, of course, long gone. He planned to get out of the area as soon as possible and get back to his duties with the gang. Carlito, however, was watching closely and managed to follow the women without getting spotted.

The first surprise was bad: the ladies were apparently lost. Eleanor missed the assigned trailhead. Carlito followed along behind the growing number of hikers. There were Angela and Eleanor, followed by Cabrito, Diego, Manuel and Pablo. They were followed by Carlito.

It was clear that Carlito and Eleanor figured out what was up long before Angela and the Keystone kidnappers.

Eleanor led them to marker 13, or *trece en Español*, in a mostly deserted area. Cabrito pulled out his Glock 9mm and told the women that they had gone far enough. He also pulled out plastic ties to handcuff them. Angela was terrified. Eleanor just said, "OK. No need to get rough We're just two women out sightseeing. You don't need to handcuff us." Diego, a little stupidly, agreed and told Cabrito to put away the Glock and handcuffs, no problem here.

Eleanor pushed Angela to the ground, reached into her backpack, drew her Beretta and kicked Cabrito in the groin area—all in a matter of seconds. Carlito appeared and disarmed the rest of the gang while Cabrito was straining to breathe.

The second surprise was worse: Juanito appeared with his Glock aimed directly at Carlito. "Hold it right there, *amigos*," ordered Juanito, addressing his gang members. Juanito complained, "I can't trust you *locos* to do anything right, so I followed you. Diego, kill the two soldiers, the woman, and the man, We will just take the gringo's lady. He'll pay plenty to get her back." Things looked as bad as possible for Eleanor and Carlito.

Surprise number three, however, wasn't bad at all. Three well-armed, tough looking Americans appeared from behind the shed at Marker number *trece* "Drop the weapons and put your hands on top of your heads or you are going to look an awful lot like Swiss *queso*," commanded the leader of the Americans. Juanito, Cabrito, Diego, Manuel and Pablo did as ordered. Those were sub-machine guns pointed at them by people who clearly knew how to use them. The American leader told Eleanor and Angela to continue their hike and enjoy the lovely Wax Palm Trees. The America team could handle the rest of the operation. Eleanor thanked her colleagues warmly but muttered to the Captain – About time you showed up, **[expletive deleted].**"

Angela heard what Eleanor said to the American leader. It had all been an American trap to capture these guys, thought Angela; and I was the bait. But it was well planned and executed, she admitted.

And so, Angela and Eleanor got back on the right trail and continued their hike in the beautiful park. The Wax Palm Trees were majestic, and Angela was very glad she had come with Charles to South America. Otherwise, she would never have met her very interesting friend Eleanor.

For many years thereafter Angela kept in touch with her new friend, who was of course, not at all what she seemed. Then Eleanor Squibb Merck vanished from the face of the earth only to re-surface five years later as the President's nominee for Director of the Central Intelligence Agency. "Gee," Angela thought, "I know the Chief Spook of the United States."

Eleanor did call Angela after her confirmation, and they had a delightful reunion including a steak dinner in Langley in the director's private dining room. It is rumored in some Washington circles that the CIA has the best food in Washington.

Back in Bogota, Angela related her tour of the *Valle de Cocora* to Charles, who seemed not to have harbored the slighted suspicion that Carlito was a trained security operative.

But Advent wasn't quite over for Angela. She received a call from Maria Gonzales, Eleanor's assistant at the Bogota Embassy. Angela had told Eleanor about her long history in participating in Advent events, including writing several Advent pageants. Eleanor told Maria, who was the wife of the Revered Benito Gonzales, Pastor of the Bogota Wesleyan Church about one of Angela's Advent stories. Reverend Benito, as he liked to be called, had always wanted to present an Advent program and thought Angela might be the answer to his prayers.

Maria asked Angela if she would lend Maria one of her Advent stories for Maria to read to the children of her church Maria said she would also very much appreciate Angela's attendance at the program, with Charles, too, of course.

Angela readily agreed. She and Charles showed up at five o'clock for the children's program. When it was over, about thirty minutes later, the *niños* gathered around Angela and one by one gave Angela a wonderful Christmas present that year – a big, big hug.

When the last child paid her respects, Angela felt her heart strangely warmed and whispered to Charles – "What a wonderful Christmas present this has been, and I think I may have another wonderful Christmas present, too." Charles, being nobody's fool, almost keeled over at that comment.

June rolled around; and it was time for Charles and Angela, clearly with child, as the Bible puts it, to return to America.

While they would be happy to resume their American life, neither Charles nor Angela would ever forget Columbia in their hearts.

For certain—Angela would never forget the *Valle de Cocora* and her adventure in South America.

CHAPTER 9

ANGELA'S REWARD

 Angela Henderson was busily work-
ing on her church's annual Christmas pag-
eant when the telephone interrupted her.
"Now what?" thought Angela, somewhat
peeved. For many years, the Advent season
had always kept Angela fully occupied. As a
child, she had performed in several pageant; as an older
youth, Angela had proved herself an able director; and
now as a young Mom, she was going to limit herself to a
short skit at the end of the New Canaan United Methodist
Church's annual Christmas event.

Angela's church divided its pageant twofold. The
first segment consisted of an outdoor drama with a few
real animals but mostly with children and youth dressed
up in colorful animal costumes. The pastor, Dr. Ted Walther liked to play the role of Gabriel, expanded to a considerable length. Gabriel was more like a master of cere-
monies than a proclaimer of glad tidings.

It was often bone-chilling cold in Connecticut during the Advent season Sometimes snow showers accompanied the frigid weather. This season was no exception;
it was cold, cold in lower New England and the snow was
falling in near record levels.

The second part of the event took place inside.
"Thank heavens,", mused Angela. She would present a
skit for the children, entitled "The Parable of the Birds,"
by Louis Cassels. It was an old skit, written nearly a

century ago. Angela had kept the weathered old story poster boards from her youth. Angela's Mom had presented the skit several times in Angela's childhood church, Abington United Methodist Church. Abington was located in upstate New York and gave New Canaan a run for its money as to which had the harshest winters Abington usually won.

All these things ran through Angela's mind as she raced for the telephone. Her husband, Charles Henderson, was on a trip for his company and the call might be from him. Charles didn't like to be away from home during the Advent season, but he reported directly to the President of his corporation, and Charles had to go when and where he was sent. This time he was traveling in the Middle East, always a potential flashpoint of troublesome politics.

Angela answered eagerly, expecting Charles on the other end of the line. It was Lois O'Reilly, Dr. Williams' administrative assistant. Angela knew Lois casually and knew Charles thought the world of her. Lois was a great administrative assistant. She was efficient to the nth degree, and a very nice person as well. Lois asked Angela to hold a moment while she got Dr Williams on the phone. Now Angela was worried; Dr. Williams was very down to Earth but a business titan, and didn't usually call his employees' family members. Dr, Williams got on the line and wasted no time.

"Angela, I have some bad news for you, but want you to know we will do everything we can to help Charles," said Dr. Williams. Then Angela learned that a tribal Chieftain in some remote corner of the Middle East had decided to kidnap some American and make an example of him. Charles had been chosen for this honor.

Dr. Williams said that their information was that Charles was in good health and that the Chieftain was likely going to make a few headlines and then turn Charles loose. But you never know, and things can get out of hand quickly in such a situation. The American Embassy was in touch with national leaders, but the national leaders weren't necessarily in touch with the tribal leaders. Dr. Williams said that they had a DVD of Charles having coffee with the local leaders and that Charles had used a pre-arranged signal to indicate that he was doing okay. Dr, Williams said that the situation could be much worse, but that they weren't underestimating the risks involved. These people carry big, curved weapons and know how to use them. Angela asked Dr. Williams if the tribe was asking for anything in particular. Well, said Dr, Williams, please keep this confidential, but they want twenty million dollars as a show good faith. Likely, they will ask for other things in addition to good faith. We have to be sure we are talking to the people who can make things happen, such as Charles' release.

As Angela hung up from her call from Dr. Williams, Charles was contemplating his future with "The Shining Light Forces" of Abdul Bin Assad, a local potentate. Charles noted that Abdul sported a spectacular beard and a very large, curved knife and did, indeed, look like he knew how to wield the business end of same.

"Er, Sheik Abdul," ventured Charles, "Have you received any communication from my company?"

"No, infidel" responded Abdul in a tone of voice that discouraged further comment. Abdul did not intimidate our hero however, as Charles decided he would test this guy's mettle.

"Look, Sheik Abdul," retorted Charles. "I don't see what good sequestering me is going to do your cause. I'm not a technical man and wouldn't know one oil sand from another. I'm just a lawyer."

"Silence! American dog, before I lose my patience and let my men work you over head to toe."

"Yeah," Charles said, "A lot of good that will do your cause whatever it is. We have a long memory in Hexi-All and we don't like to see our employees mistreated. I'm not sure you have enough sand to protect your tribe if we decide to come after you." Charles was mad now, and he know Dr. Williams wouldn't take the kidnapping of one of his people lightly. It's true Hexi-All doesn't have an army; but that didn't mean they couldn't rent one. Abdul seemed to weigh Charles' outburst with some respect.

Meanwhile, Dr. Williams called his emergency team into session, and they proceeded to scope out the problem and what they might do about this considerable affront. Also, Dr Williams was determined to get Charles back without too much wear and tear on Charles. One crusty up streamer said, "Let's just hire a helicopter assault team and go get him, I'll be glad to go along for the ride." Actually, nobody objected, but an airborne assault might endanger Charles to the extreme. The money people thought why not pay the ransom, it wasn't that much money. However, Dr. Williams thought to himself, "Yeah but turning over that much money to a bandit might ruin Charles' future, as well as endanger him again." People would always think: Was this guy really worth $20 million? Furthermore, how come he was dumb enough to get captured by a bunch of third world bandits, Such a view would demean people who had centuries of experience at banditry. But the public often shows an amazing lack of understanding when it comes to things like history.

One public affairs type said, "Let's see what our government thinks we should do. Not a single attendee other that the proponent liked that idea at all. The current US president wasn't much in the courage department and would probably just refer them to the good-for-nothing State Department. Besides, Hexi-All had as good intelligence sources as the State Department. True, the kidnappers weren't much in the sophistication department either, but they did know how to shoot AK-47s and other such armaments. Charles' life was foremost in Dr. Williams' thought.

Angela had a lot of confidence in Charles' employer, but she couldn't help being scared witless. The corporate name derived from the old name, Hexi Oil Company. The Hexi represented the six continents with company operations. When alternative energy sources and uses came along, the name was changed to Hexi-All Corporation.

Angela was aware that a rich Texan had bank-rolled a rescue operation in a similar situation, and she knew that Hexi-All had a lot more resources at its finger-tips than the billionaire. She also knew that Charles was a cool customer and might just talk himself out of a very tight spot.

So, she willed herself to think about the annual Christmas event at her church, She could do the Parable of the Birds skit blindfolded. But she had also been drafted to direct the rest of the inside program. The pastor would direct the outside segment. Out in the court-yard, **The Fair Apple and Cider Farm** had loaned the church a live sheep or two as well as a cow to enliven the sound effects. There would be real baas and maybe even some lowing to accompany Dr. Walther. The camels, oxen and donkeys would have to be live human players. Dr. Walther prided himself on his Latin and Hebrew; so he would do the Mishnah and throw in a few Latin phrases, as well. He was of Italian extraction on his mother's side, and by golly he was going to speak some Latin, He had gone to Yale Divinity School and was very proud of his classical language skills. It isn't clear what the Mishnah has to do with the Christmas story, but the pastor liked to hear his own resonant, but clipped, New England Hebrew. He could just imagine everyone gasp-ing in awe as he called: "Hear, O Israel..." in Hebrew, of course.

Angela's little girl, Margaret, wanted to know when Daddy would be back from his trip; and Angela greatly feared that the kidnappers would make a public pitch for their cause and identify their victim publicly. Angela's situation was bad enough without having a four-year-old scared to death for her Father. Little Susannah was too young to understand the situation but would certainly pick up on Angela's and her big sister's fears— not an easy time for Angela. Like the first century of Baby Jesus' era, life was risky and full of danger in Angela's world. People still killed for political purposes.

By now Charles had figured out that he was intended as a mere figurehead in Abdul's game plan. "I don't like being this guy's pawn to be sacrificed when he thinks opportune," thought Charles. Charles understood a little Arabic and had figured out that he was to be moved to one of Abdul's rundown cities near the Gulf. Some third cousin was to have the opportunity of hosting a very unwilling guest. The city was large enough for a possible escape. By now Charles had enough facial hair and a sufficient suntan to pass for a local if he could make his escape. Abdul's cousin was a long way from a rocket scientist, but he had a mean looking AK-47 and loved shooting it into the air. Every now and then bullets, amazingly enough fell from the sky and created a few more martyrs.

But the cousin had a very intelligent son who wanted no part of a captured American who had high standing in one of the world's largest corporations with a reputation for taking care of its own. Plus, the son hated Abdul with a passion that grew out of a personal issue that he would never discuss. A chance at revenge and removing a threat to his own family might just prove irresistible. Allies come from strange and unexpected places at times. Still Charles had no reasonable hope for help from such an unexpected place. He was to be proved very wrong.

Dr Williams' people were working day and night trying to set up a channel of communications with Abdul. Actually, US governmental help was offered and accepted. It turned out the governmental sources did have better intelligence than the corporate world, and the government was willing to share the intelligence in this case. Abdul was a threat to way too many people, and this would help Charles enormously.

One governmental agent who liked to go by the name of Mahmoud knew Abdul's relations in the town where Charles was being held. Mahmoud knew that the cousin was afraid of Abdul, but the cousin's son hated Abdul with a passion akin to recklessness. If Charles was being held by Abdul or the cousin, there was a chance of some undercover help.

Hexi-All's Chief of Security, John Smith [That was really his name; although it is doubtful that Mahmoud was really the name of the government agent], met with Mahmoud in Dubai's magnificent new hotel. They agreed on a plan that was worthy of Ian Fleming's James Bond. There would be a secret approach to Charles's captors and a deal cut. What should happen to Abdul was left to his relatives, but it would not likely be pretty. He had taken advantage of his cousin's daughter and there were clear signs of repayment time at the oasis.

Of course, Angela knew nothing of the details of Charles' confinement. She just knew she wanted Charles back for Christmas time in New England. She had two little daughters, and they needed their father. Besides, she was worried sick personally. She rehearsed her skit over and over again. Margaret was so pleased with the story and particularly the clever Posters of Birds. The story is a little worrisome because of the plight of the poor birds. We can only hope the birds get the message somehow.

A few days later, still no word from Charles. But also, no public word from the bandits who had captured Charles. That is a little unusual. Why haven't they come out with their news and demands for the release of Charles? Dr. Williams had called twice to say that things were looking up with regard to Charles' situation, but he could say no more.

Now it is almost time for the Christmas Eve Pageant. Sure enough, it is cold and snowing hard. The outside contingent was wearing very warm clothing.

It is eleven o'clock in the evening and Dr. Walther is about to recite his Hebrew exhortation to Israel, and New Canaan United Methodist church-goers out in the courtyard. After the Pastor calls on the true believers to harken to the one true God, he recites a bit of the KJV of the Luke Christmas story He even throws in some Latin. There were a few angels, some animals, and of course the family in the stable. We have to wait a few days for the Wise Men, but we know they are coming.

Shaking off the numbing cold, everyone went into the Fellowship Hall to hear the inside pageant. The rest of the Luke story is read. There are a few other preliminaries before Angela gets to do her skit.

Then quietly settling into the back row is a bearded thirty-something man surrounded by what look like Secret Service agents. They are all wearing little earpieces with a coiled wire running down the neck. The beaded man doesn't seem to have one though.

As Angela gets up to give her rendition of the *Parable of the Birds*, her eyes settle on the bearded stranger. She lets out a radiant smile that confuses the Pastor and the other congregants. All is clear however, when little Margaret [who has been allowed to stay up just this once to hear her Mommy] runs back to hug the bearded stranger. The men with the earpieces, not normally known for their sense of humor, smile and let her through.

With a renewed sense of what is right with the world, Angela goes up front and begins her story of:

"The Parable of the Birds"
by Louis Cassels

And as Angela concluded her story of the birds, Charles stood up in the back of the church and applauded, All the assembled children were delighted with Angela's story. And from far away on his heavenly perch Gabriel smiled at his favorite human being.

CHAPTER 10

ANGELA'S *NIGHTMARE* BEFORE CHRISTMAS

It was the best of times; it was the worst of times. That immortal catchphrase hammered constantly in Angela Henderson's head. "Go away, Charles Dickens, and never come back," ordered Angela to no one in particular. She was in charge of writing the script for her church's annual Christmas pageant, and words were not flowing forth. She hadn't been able to find an opening line, much less an immortal catchphrase.

She looked at the blank page on her computer and thought: I'll never finish this script on time. It was due on the Wednesday after Thanksgiving; and that was only ten days away. Angela and her husband Charles and their young children, Margaret and Susannah, were active members of New Canaan United Methodist Church, and Angela did not like to disappoint anyone. She particularly hated to let down her Pastor, Reverend Ted Walther.

All she could think about were the opening lines of Dicken's great novel, *A Tale of Two Cities*. Reminds me of Beethoven's Fifth Symphony, she thought. Who could force that musical masterpiece out of one's mind? Or the old knock, knock joke—"Knock, knock—Who's there?" However, the answer to her knock, knock question was: nothing is there. No creativity, no flowing prose, nothing.

As she was trying desperately to stop feeling sorry for herself, sure enough, someone was at the door.

The call was a doorbell, not a knock, knock, but the effect was the same. Angela snapped out of her reverie and went into her "thirty-something housewife mode."

"Coming," Angela called out. The news would not be good.

Wearing a bright yellow rain slicker and a somber expression was the husband of Angela's acquaintance Maria Giulia. Captain Georgio Giulia was head of the New Canaan, Connecticut, Child Protection Service – he was truly one of New Canaan's finest.

"Mrs. Henderson," said the Captain. "I have some disturbing news, may I come in?"

"Certainly," responded Angela, "and please call me Angela. I have done some PTA work at Center School with your wife, Maria."

"Thank you," responded Captain Giulia. "I won't take up much of your time, but I feel that the parents of the neighborhood children need to be well informed when there is a risk to their children's safety."

Well, that comment certainly alarmed Angela. She worried some about her husband's safety. Charles flew all around the world for Hexi-All Corporation. He regularly went to countries where some of the natives carried big knives in their belts, and Charles said they knew how to use them, too. But there is nothing like a threat to one's children to drive a dagger of fear right through the heart.

"What do you mean, Captain?" asked Angela with a note of fear in her voice.

"We believe that there has been a stalker in your neighborhood, Angela, and we are determined to do everything we can to protect our children. I have no doubt we will apprehend him, but we plan to take no chances with the children. Do you mind if I see that your children are safe?"

"Not at all," responded Angela. Margaret is 7 and Susannah is 4 and both are in the game room with their new nanny, Mary Hopkins. The kids call her Mary Poppins, when she's not around. Follow me."

However, neither the nanny not the kids were there when Angela, followed by the Captain, opened the door to the Game Room. "That's funny, said Angela. Where could they be?"

There was a door to the outside from the Game Room, and it was slightly ajar. "They shouldn't be out in this cold drizzle," said Angela a bit angry. But there they were in one corner of Angela's spacious backyard, all bundled up like two little Eskimos. However, Mary Poppins was nowhere to be seen.

"Where's Mary?" asked Angela, thoroughly frightened by now. Margaret, the older daughter answered: "Oh, she left with Harry to go get their car. They told us they'd be right back to take us for a ride in their new car. Then they saw the Police cars drive up and they ran off in that direction," added Margaret pointing toward the alley.

That was enough for Captain Giulia He walked away from Angela and the girls and spoke briefly into his shoulder mike. He looked excited and a little grim, noticed Angela. She would look back on this event and thank the good Lord over and over for Captain Giulia's unexpected visit. She also vowed to do a better job of screening the next nanny.

When he returned to the group, Captain Giulia suggested that they all go back into the house and maybe Angela would make the girls some hot chocolate while he made some calls on his cellphone, and then he said privately to Angela that he needed to talk with her about Mary Hopkins or whatever her real name was.

After about 30 minutes, Captain Giulia and Angela had their talk. Angela produced Mary's employment application, including a copy of her Connecticut driver's license, her W-9 IRS form which included a social security number, and 3 or 4 solid references. "Looks in order," said the Captain, "but forgers are very clever these day." Sure enough, Mary Hopkins or the kids' Mary Poppins was a total phony, and her boyfriend was a registered sex offender in three states. He is a hot suspect for the stalker, but that case is still open.

What is clear is that Angela's two girls had a narrow escape from a potentially awful experience – talk about "A Nightmare Before Christmas." Angela and Charles suffered a few nightmares of their own over the years when they thought back about their close call.

Some years are better than others, this is not to be one of the better ones for Angela. One nightmare may be over, but Angela isn't through with the potential nightmares looming this Advent season. Plus, Angela has writer's block and can't get started on her Advent story.

Maybe right now is just the worst of times, thought Angela. Perhaps the best of times were all in the past, or they are going to happen in the future.

Four days, including Thanksgiving, passed. Angela was so scared by the close call her daughters faced with almost being kidnapped that she snapped out of her funk and actually finished about half of her Advent pageant "Well done, Angela, said Pastor Ted Walther when she told him of her progress, "You have the ability to take an old, old story and make it fresh and exciting. Not many people can do that."

Angela was very pleased with her pastoral praise, but she was only five days away from her deadline.

The phone rang, and Angela started. She was a little nervous these days when the unexpected happened, It was Captain Giulia. The police had found Mary Hopkins, which turned out to be her real name, to Julia's surprise. She was with Harry.

Her boyfriend and accomplice was one Harold Hill. Yes, that was his real name too, and he wasn't a music man. Hill was wanted in New York for child endangerment. There were several other criminal warrants for his arrest outstanding. It seems he had been "married" three times in the Bahamas without going to the trouble of getting a divorce or annulment. In other words, as the understating British would say: He was a thorough scoundrel. With respect to Hill's one legitimate marriage, not to Mary Hopkins, he had outstanding warrants for spousal abuse and nonpayment of support.

Nonetheless Mary stood by him and was about to join him in a serious felony by kidnapping Angela's two children. Captain Giulia's only comment to Angela was, "Poor Mary, some women never learn." Angela bristled at that comment—a bit sexist there, Captain. It should be: some people never learn.

Angela identified Mary Hopkins and was prepared to testify against her. Mary, now thoroughly frightened and freed from Hill's bondage, turned state's evidence on Mr. Harold Hill. His goose was cooked, thought Angela.

The Captain was very pleased with that aspect of the case but was still concerned about the neighborhood stalker. Hill had a rock-solid alibi as to the known dates the alleged stalker was stalking. Hill was in the New Haven municipal lockup and nowhere near New Canaan when the offense occurred.

So, who was lurking in the bushes, scaring the townsfolk, if it wasn't Harold Hill?

Angela and Charles were discussing the Hill/Hopkins case and the unknown stalker situation, having no idea that little Margaret was listening to their conversation. About the time they had worked themselves up into a state of anxiety over the stalker, Margaret moved out from behind the couch and said, "Oh, that's just Boo Radley, playing Halloween."

"Margaret, Boo Radley is a character from the movie *To Kill a Mockingbird; he is not a real person*," said Angela, with a note of annoyance, In truth, she was more than a little annoyed with herself for not sensing Margaret's presence. She and Charles would never have knowingly discussed the Hill case or the stalker in front of their children.

"I know that," answered Margaret, a little annoyed that her mother thought her so dumb. But Eddie Heever down the street likes to dress up like Boo on Halloween and scare the kids in the neighborhood, Charles and Angela were very familiar with and liked the Heever family, and knew that thirteen-year-old Edward Heever had some issues similar to those of the fictional Boo, and he seemed good natured. While something of a loner, Eddie was thought not likely to harm anyone. *Could the mystery be this easily solved?*

Charles called Captain Giulia and told him what Margaret had said—that the whole incident may be totally innocent. Julia said he certainly hoped this was true—especially with everyone on edge about the Hill case. We shall see.

The creative juices were now flowing in Angela's veins. She was almost through writing the pageant and had three days until the deadline. Nothing could stop her now. She was on a roll.

Bad things come in threes, they say. First came the near abduction; then the unsolved stalker incident. What else could possibly happen?

The lights could go out in New Canaan and they did. The heavens had opened and it had been raining almost continuously for three days It had rained over 10 inches in 72 hours. The ground was soaked and, in a town noted for its large trees, they were falling right and left.

The power company had its own nightmare before Christmas.

Angela was putting the finishing touches to her manuscript when she heard a loud pop. Then the lights flickered; then half her house went dark. The other half grew dim as though a ghostly rheostat was controlling the electricity. She hastily printed out her manuscript. Page 98 emerged from the old Hewlett-Packard just as the rest of the house lost all power She was saved but for what? Lost in darkness.

Charles went out front where the New England Power and Light Company people were working on the nearby transformer. The power company had appeared during the latest lull in the rainstorm. Charles was holding a large lantern for one of the workers who was outfitted with huge rubber gloves and an insulated suit. Charles was a bit nervous with the exposed wires: he had never seen any electrical wiring of the size the tech was holding—huge, number 4 wiring according to the tech.

Suddenly, there was a flash of light that looked like a phosphorus shell exploding between Charles and the worker, exceeded in excitement only by the loud explosive pop.

When Charles' vision returned, he asked the worker if he was all right, fully thinking the tech had been fried to a crisp. "Yeah, but that is enough excitement for me for a while," the electrician proclaimed.

Charles thought the better part of wisdom would be to spend a night or two at the local hotel, notably named the Roger Sherman Inn. Fortunately, there were two rooms left, and Charles gratefully grabbed them. Under the hotel rules, Charles had to occupy one room and Angela the other. The younger daughter stayed with Angela and Margaret claimed her father as her roommate.

The Roger Sherman Inn was on a different power grid from the rest of New Canaan. It was the only place in town with electricity However it served only adult food; and about ten that night the family was hungry for more mundane fare. Charles got in the car and retrieved some cans of Vienna Sausages and hot dog buns. Not fancy, but memorable for years thereafter.

That night Margaret got up to go to the bathroom and almost in a sleepwalking state walked right out the room. The door locked behind her. Her father was sound asleep, and he couldn't hear her knocking. Margaret tried the door to the next room, but it was of course locked. She was trapped in the hallway. She started crying and someone heard her and asked which was her room. She pointed out her and Charles' room. The next Charles heard was a gruff voice and a loud knocking at his door. He let Margaret back in with many thanks to the sleepy man who had rescued her.

The power returned to the Henderson house after two nights at the Roger Sherman Inn. The sojourn had been pleasant enough, but the family was glad to be back home.

It turned out that the local Boo Radley had been innocently spooking the neighborhood by rustling in the bushes and looking for his fictional friend, Scout Finch. Mr. Heever managed to convince Boo/Edward that he should only scare people on Halloween and not hide in the bushes of his friends' homes. The police got rave newspaper notices for catching Harold Hill; and Boo was let off with a mild reprimand by Judge Albritton, the Municipal Judge.

Judge Albritton was chairman of the deacons of the First Baptist Church of New Canaan, and the locals would prefer jailtime to listening to one of his admonitions of faith in Church or reprimands in court. There was little difference in the two. Separation of Church and State did not apply in Brother Albritton's courtroom. The Writ of the United States Supreme Court did not extend to the chambers of Thomas Jefferson Albritton, presiding Judge of the Municipal Court and the Juvenile Court of New Canaan, Connecticut.

Angela was pleased with the rehearsals for the annual Christmas Pageant at the New Canaan United Methodist Church this year. Pastor Walther said her manuscript was the best ever and that the director and actors were inspired by her writing. Rev. Walther was a bit of a ham himself and loved his role in the Pageant.

Christmas Eve found Angela in an extraordinarily good mood. The congregation was excitedly expectant. The weather was mild.

The Pageant started on time. All the actors, young and old, did their parts the best Angela had ever experienced, Rev. Walther showed off his knowledge of Hebrew by reciting the *Shema* in Hebrew, of course. [*Shema:* "Hear, O Israel, the Lord is our God."]

In the outdoor part of the pageant, there were real donkeys and sheep from the Fair Farm, which provided the animals as well as apple cider. The cow was a little scrawny, but the shepherds and angels made up for that minor inadequacy.

At the precise moment of midnight, the full moon cast a beam of light on the doll that represent the baby Jesus and the whole congregation broke into song:

"Silent night, holy night. All is calm, all is bright."

Yes, thought Angela. It is the best of times. Merry Christmas to one and all.

CHAPTER 11:

GABRIEL'S MISSION

 Gabriel is God's right-hand angel; and at the moment the archangel is very, very busy. His main job is to take on important missions for the Almighty. But he also watches over a list of God's children who are fortunate enough to be assigned to him. Of all the people Gabriel protects, none is more precious to him than Angela Trufelli Henderson. Gabriel has looked after her since she was eight; and he plans to do so for the rest of her earthly life.

The other archangels are a little envious of Gabriel's and Angela's mutual attachment, but they dearly love Gabriel and bear him no ill will. There is even speculation that: as Angela is Gabriel's favorite human, so is Gabriel God's favorite archangel. But that never bothers the other six: Suruel, Raphael, Raguel, Michael, Remiel and Uriel. [In fairness, there are other lists with different names for the seven.]

Angela, on the other hand, isn't much bothered about anything today. As the calendar turns to December, she reflects on her great life in New Canaan, Connecticut. At the moment, she is busily working on the script for the New Canaan Methodist Church's annual Christmas pageant. She has written so many of these stories that she is sure she could script one blindfolded.

Her elder daughter, Margaret, is playing Gabriel in the pageant this year; and that alone brings back a flood of beautiful memories. Angela played the archangel Gabriel in her first speaking role in her home church's pageant over two decades ago. It was the occasion of her introduction to the archangel himself. Gabriel said she was the best Gabriel ever.

Now, Angela writes the script for the pageant, and she is breezing through the entire task. "And it came to pass in those days, that a decree went out ..." she said quietly. Gabriel [who can be anywhere] was in a sense reading the script over her shoulder – unbeknownst to Angela. Of course.

"Not half bad," thought Gabriel. As he finished page 10. But Gabriel had to abandon his editorializing upon being summoned to a conference with God and the man with the kind face.

"Ah, Gabriel, there you are," said the man with the kind face. "We need your unique talent, there is a huge storm brewing out in the Atlantic, and it bodes ill for your beloved Angela."

New Canaan, the State of Connecticut, or for that matter, all of New England can be cold and dreary in late Fall. This year was the exception—or it had been until now. Angela thought that God had smiled particularly on her neck of the woods this year, weather-wise. On occasion, an early New England storm covers the area with a beautiful blanket of pristine snow. Angela had commented to Charles over breakfast how mild this fall had been.

Angela was looking forward to a pre-Christmas trip to London for a week's visit with an SMU sorority sister. Her friend's husband, Bill, works for Hexi-All Corporation where Angela's husband also earns his daily bread. Charles is higher on the pecking order, but Bill is doing well in the Exploration Department. Sally and Bill Angle were transferred to London the past summer; and Sally is more than a little homesick. Sally is tall, blonde and hails from Midland, Texas—a long haul from England, even though Midland claims to be an oasis of culture on the West Texas frontier. Bill is tall, redheaded, and Sally would say enormously handsome. He is a Highland Park, Texas, native who was a basketball star at Southern Methodist University. In his day, he was considered the Doak Walker of basketball—well, almost. Angela has a fertile imagination.

Bill is having the time of his life, travelling all over Europe, Africa, and the Middle East. Petroleum exploration is just that, you have to explore, often in difficult and remote places if you are hunting for "elephants." That quaint term is used by the big companies to describe the size of the petroleum fields they need.to find to keep their reserves level or ahead of depletion, The reserves in the longed-for fields have a lot of zeroes after that first digit.

Bill is a great husband and father, but like many corporate executives somewhat insensitive to the difficulties of a corporate transfer on the rest of the family. Sally was a very good soldier, as they say in the corporate world, and was in most ways enjoying her role as an expat in a very desirable location.

The A+ Limo Company picked Angela up at her side door at exactly 5:00 pm for the 90-minute ride to JFK airport, Charles came home early to see Angela off. He was a close friend of both Bill and Sally and was a little sad that he couldn't go with Angela. But he knew this was Angela's pre-Christmas present, and he was very happy for the two girls, as he put it.

Lift-off for transatlantic flight 0080 on British Airways was scheduled for 9:00 PM; so Angela had plenty of time to relax at the American Airlines Admirals Club. Charles had surprised Angela with a club membership last year, and she was rather enjoying her lapse into luxury in the club lounge.

The Boeing 787 lifted off about thirty minutes late and after a slight turn headed North and East for Terminal 5 of London's Heathrow Airport. The pilot knew that a storm was brewing over the North Atlantic and his flight plan brought 0080 North of the turbulence. In fact, he was directed to fly very near Iceland.

The Danes, as one branch of the Vikings, had discovered, Iceland long before Columbus sailed the ocean blue. While the Vikings had a bad reputation as good neighbors, they were plenty smart. They named a nice little island with many thermal springs and a very livable environment – Iceland. Who would want to invade an island of ice? The western and much larger island was just barely habitable, which they adroitly named Greenland. Greenland was truly almost all ice and rock. The Vikings also were careful to give the towns of Iceland such names as Reykjavik or some other unspeakable name that the Vikings hoped might discourage invasion.

As a lark, Charles had given Angela a DNA testing kit through Ancestry.com. Her maiden name was Tru-felli; and her family had a distinct Italian flavor, She knew she would test 100% Italian, but to her surprise, she had a 10% Scandinavian and 35% Irish DNA reading. Many Irish, of course, have Viking ancestors. Perhaps that helps explain Angela's beautiful blonde hair and clear blue eyes.

Angela took her revenge on Charles and bought him an Ancestry.com DNA kit. You might think Hender-son would rank high on the Viking curve, but Charles turned out to be almost entirely Western Europe, that is French and West German. You just never know, mused Angela to Charles' chagrin.

Back to our transatlantic flight: Angela had splurged and bought a business class ticket. So, about midnight Connecticut time, she maneuvered the lay-flat seat into an almost horizontal mode. It wasn't easy get-ting the seat just right. She let out at least one very un-characteristic expletive in the process, but the seats were far enough apart that the comment went unregistered by her seatmates – or so she hoped. Angela settled in for a calm and uneventful sleep.

The storm moved toward Flight 0080 and was much more severe and widespread than expected. The *Fasten Seat Belt* sign flashed on, not that everyone wasn't already buckled up. The copilot came on the intercom and gave the standard speech about encountering some turbulence and would everyone please return to their seats if they weren't in them, fasten their seat belts, etc. What a nice calm voice, thought Angela.

The storm struck. The thunderclouds rose 50,000 feet in the air, well above the normal flight pattern of commercial airlines. The Boeing 787 is an extraordinarily safe aircraft. It has been designed to take a good deal of buffeting about. The human nervous system, however, acts up when tossed about like a salad at approximately 40,000 feet up in the air. Angela is not the nervous type, but this was getting scary. The airplane shook and rumbled; lightning flashed; and loud noises abounded.

The Captain came back on the intercom and announced that they were going to make an unexpected landing at Keflavik Airport, another of those unspeakable Icelandic names. Headwinds had caused an unexpected usage of fuel, and the Pilot thought best to seek shelter. Keflavik was an hour and a half away – if he put the pedal to the metal. Angela thought that the pilot should save his humor for a later date. "Pedal to the Metal," indeed, she murmured.

Some thirty minutes from Iceland, one of the two giant engines quit on them. The co-pilot saw no need to announce the latest problem. But the cockpit recorder caught the flight deck discussion; and it was not reassuring. Running through Angela's mind was the old John Wayne movie, *The High and the Mighty*. Angela could empathize with the altitude part of the title; but she certainly didn't feel mighty.

About that moment, Angela, now that the seats were in their upright and locked position, glanced over and saw a figure in a brilliantly bright white outfit quite unusual for a businessman headed for London. She gasped when she recognized her neighbor. "Gabriel, is that you?" asked Angela.

"Yep, it's me," was the response.

"What are you doing here?" she asked.

"Thought you might like a little company" was the answer. "Also, I have some suggestions for your Advent Pageant," he craftily suggested.

"Are you nuts?" came her response. "We [not you, of course] are about to die and you want to talk Advent?"

Gabriel chuckled. "I can't change the course of human history, as you know, but I've been known to steer it a little," said Gabriel. "I do know that we are going to land somewhat as planned in Iceland; but there will be some bigtime problems," added Gabriel.

The pilot turned to the co-pilot and said, "Thank God, there are the landing lights."

The Co-pilot responded, "Looks like a sea of mud down there." As they touched down on the edge of the runway, a massive windshear hit the plane broadside and the aircraft veered to the side of the runway. Then off the runway onto the gravel, and then onto a strip of muddy grass – or more aptly a strip of grassy mud. As the plane came to an abrupt stop in the gooey stuff, the landing gear collapsed. Some of the passengers had been severely tossed about, and a row of seats nearly broke free.

Angela had a mild head injury, but some of the passengers were hurt worse.

The airport authorities summoned several ambulances, and the airplane crew did a magnificent job evacuating the injured passengers from the damaged aircraft. Angela was taken to a hospital for inspection. Her seatmate was nowhere to be found.

The hospital staff did the routine work up. Do you know what day this is, one asked; Angela answered correctly. Do you know who the US President is; she answered correctly. What is your Name? Angela went blank. She didn't know who she was.

"How is everyone?" asked Angela, thoughtful as always. "Some of the passengers and crew are injured," replied the Icelandic doctor assigned to treat Angela, "But thank heaven, no one was killed." Dr Amberg added. "You have no external injuries that we have discovered, and for that matter, no internal injuries that have showed up on our imaging devices." Dr. Amberg then disclosed what she feared most: "You seem to have some sort of trauma-induced amnesia. By the way, we know your name is Angela Henderson."

However induced, Angela wanted no part of any condition that blanked out her memory. The strange part of it was that she remembered that she was married to a wonderful man, had two beautiful daughters, and a great life somewhere in the colder part of America—she wasn't quite sure where, though—perhaps in Upper New York State. She also remembered that she had a good friend named Gabriel, but she wasn't quite sure what he looked like or how he fit into her life.

Gabriel, watching all this from his heavenly perch, was distraught. He had done all he could to save Angela and the others on the plane, and thank God, he had succeeded on that part. But his beloved Angela was stuck in a hospital in Iceland and temporarily unable to even remember her name. What a sad Christmas this was turning out to be.

The man with the kind face found Gabriel pacing up and down the streets of gold. Gabriel had always thought that the human description of Heaven was a serious oversell. The streets were not made of gold and the gates were not pearly; in fact, there were no gates. But many centuries ago, an inspired human tried to describe his vision of heaven and that was the most wonderful scene he could imagine.

"Have you thought of some plan to rescue Angela?" asked the man with the kind face.

"Not yet," responded Gabriel.

"Perhaps she will recover on her own," mused the man with the kind face. Gabriel thought that such a recovery would be just like Angela, but he dreaded the thought that she might not be able to overcome her problems on her own.

In the meantime, Dr. Amberg decided to remove Angela from the hospital and take her home to be with his family so she could have some companionship and he could observe her in a non-clinical environment. Dr Amberg's wife, Ursula, would be delighted to help this most pleasant American. He thought his children would like her too. Their twin daughters, Sonja and Tanya were eight and would be thrilled as well.

Angela accepted Dr. Amberg's offer immediately. Mrs. Amberg drove Angela to their home in Reykjavik that afternoon. The twins were very excited to meet their guest from America. Dr. and Mrs. Amberg came from Sweden and they were dedicated Lutherans. The Amberg family was very active in the Christ the King Church located a few blocks from the Amberg home. The girls told Angela that they had friends in the local Methodist Church who were talking about their upcoming Advent Pageant.

That comment stirred something in Angela's brain, but she couldn't quite bring the nascent thought to the surface. "Tell me all about it," said Angela, excitedly.

"Well, the Methodist Pageant tells the story of the coming of the Christ child; and there are children dressed in all kinds of costumes," said Sonja.

"Yeah, and a bunch of animals, too," and Tanya.

'No camels though," said Sonja sadly.

"We don't have any real camels, either, said Angela. "Although I think people dressed as camels come with the wise men somewhat later." There was some surprise in Angela's voice that she knew that.

"Have you been in Advent Pageants?" asked Sonja.

"Yes, I think so," responded Angela. "Yes, I know so," she added.

Dr. Amberg took off the next day, too. Life is a bit more relaxed in Iceland than in the New York area, thought Angela when Dr. Amberg told her he was taking another day off. But by doing so, Dr. Amberg observed Angela in one of her most characteristic modes – a compassionate and helpful person.

The friends of the Amberg children came over early the next morning to see the twins and the American visitor, The little Icelandic Methodists came with their mother. The family, originally from England, is part of a small group of Methodists found in largely Lutheran Iceland. As the conversation progressed, the mother asked Angela if she had participated in any Christmas plays in America. "Oh, yes." Remembered Angela "I once played the part of Gabriel in a midnight Christmas Pageants."

In an unobtrusive manner, Dr. Amberg was listening to Angela recount this part of her past. "Very good, very good." analyzed Dr. Amberg. "She is definitely regaining her memory."

True to form, Angela's helpful nature came to the surface, "Can I help you with your pageant?" she volunteered.

"Of course, we'd love to have your ideas and lean on your experience," said the Methodist mother, whose name was, of all things, Susannah—the same as Angela's younger daughter. "Lots of Methodist influence in this world," laughed Angela to herself.

"We would really like some help with the role of Gabriel in our pageant script. We just can't quite seem to get it right," said Susannah.

"Sure," said Angela, "I should be able to do that."

A little before noon the next day, Susannah came back to Dr Amberg's house to work with Angela on the script. Dr. Amberg stayed home another day because he could see that Angela was making steady progress. Right behind Susannah's arrival, however there was another ring of the Amberg doorbell. There standing in the doorway, with the Icelandic sunlight beaming directly behind him was a man dressed totally in white.

"Hello," the gleaming figure declared, "I was a passenger in Angela's airplane, seated next to her and I would like to see how she is doing."

"Come in, come in," said Dr. Amberg, eager to determine whether seeing the other passenger would help Angela. Dr. Amberg was surprised to note how bright the Sun beamed today in the little time it was allotted this time of year.

Dr. Amberg showed the unrecognized Gabriel into the living room where the pageant writers were busily scripting. "G—" was all Angela got out of her mouth before Gabriel said, "My name is Estrella and I am an old friend; I'm here to see how Angela is doing." Angela got the message that Gabriel was traveling incognito, "What are you doing, Angela?" asked Gabriel.

"Oh, just helping Susannah here with her Christmas Pageant script. We are working on the Gabriel part."

"How thoughtful of you, Angela" said Gabriel in a flattering tome, "Perhaps I can help."

"Perhaps you can," said Angela. "There is something I need to discuss with Dr. Amberg; so perhaps you can visit with Susannah while I'm gone." Gabriel took the bait and sat down by Susannah and looked over the script.

"Dr. Amberg, I am remembering some things now: my name is Angela Henderson and I live in New Canaan, Connecticut with my husband Charles. Our phone number is 203-966-1234. Could I please call him on your phone? He has probably been trying desperately to find out my location and condition."

"Of course, you may use my phone, but you won't find Charles in Connecticut. His plane arrives at Keflavik Airport tomorrow at 9:00 am. He tracked you down and is getting here as soon as humanly possible. The airport is closed until this afternoon. He is on his way." Angela just opened up and the tears rained down.

Gabriel, two rooms away, sensed the emotion felt by his beloved Angela and teared up himself. Susannah, almost as sensitive a person as Angela, noticed this and asked Gabriel if he felt alright. Gabriel was very pleased with Susannah's compassion. "Yes, I am, now," replied Gabriel. "Let's get back to your script. In fact, I have a couple of suggestions about trumpets and things."

When Angela returned to the living room, Gabriel and Susannah were having an animated discussion. Susannah was first to announce that they had finished the Gabriel part and she was enormously grateful to Angela for bringing her such an inspired script writer. "I won't change a thing your friend suggested." Susannah gushed. "He's the greatest."

"Awww," responded Gabriel with pretend modesty.

"Okay, you two, that's it," laughed Angela. "Actually, I have to fly," punned Gabriel. "I have a very important meeting to attend."

"I am so glad you're better, Angela," said Gabriel, "I'll put that in my report."

"Huh?" said Susannah, as Gabriel walked out the door.

"Oh, he likes to be mysterious," remarked Angela.

As Susannah was making her departure, she thanked Angela profusely for being so helpful. "You're welcome, Susannah, we just never know when our guardian angel, or any other messenger of hope will appear. At least, I don't; my guardian angel just materializes out of the blue when I need help."

Dr. Amberg dismissed Angela that evening but asked her to stay at his home another night He told her that he would make sure Charles knew where she was and how to get to his house.

The next morning about eleven a taxi pulled up in front of the Amberg home and a greatly relieved Charles Henderson ran to the front door. Angela beat him to it and met him on the steps. Everyone, particularly the Amberg twins, was enjoying the joyous reunion. "Now, it will be a very happy Christmas," said Charles. "We have our Angela back."

Elsewhere, the man with the kind face walked up to Gabriel and said, "You amaze me, Gabriel. You are the best. I see you have found another human in Angela's mode to look after – Susannah, eh? You seem to favor these Methodists, I note."

"Well, I think there are a lot of wonderful humans out there just like Angela and Susannah, including non-Methodists; we just need to encourage them in the Christmas spirit."

Hearing this, God smiled.

CHAPTER 12

GABRIEL VISITS
"THE NEXT STOP TO HEAVEN"

Our setting is December 2038, and we find Angela (Trufelli) Henderson crying her heart out in the sunroom of her lovely home in New Canaan, Connecticut. Snow is gently falling, and, under other circumstances, the snowfall might be a beautiful reminder of glorious Christmases gone by. This Christmas, however, will be Angela's first Christmas without Charles since before she could remember; and her pain is palpable.

Angela had tried to eat lunch, but really had just picked at her food. I must get my feelings under control, Angela orders herself. Her older daughter Margaret and husband, Pat, and their twins Marie and Grace will be arriving by A+ Limo from LaGuardia about 4 o'clock. It is almost time for the annual Christmas gathering.

Angela's middle child, Susannah, is in France with her husband of one year, Jean-Marque du Ret. The du Ret family descends from an ancient clan of distinguished Huguenots. This branch of the du Ret family returned to France from Northern Ireland upon Napoleon's ascent. Jean-Marque is serving a government internship in Paris with the American embassy. Sadly, he couldn't get away this year.

Angela's third and youngest child, Andrew, is away at prep school and will join the family tomorrow.

Angela mused to herself that her beloved baby boy was something of an afterthought—

By the time Susannah joined the family, Charles had abandoned the 51st floor of the Hexi-All building in New York City for greener pastures. He had evidently passed his training assignment, for they gave him a promotion. That was a good thing, since a four-member family is expensive in New Canaan. Charles spent a lot of time in airplanes, going here, there and everywhere in the broad expanse of Hexi-All's empire. He didn't have to join the Army to see the world. Actually, he thought, while the idea might sound romantic and exciting, travel does get tiring – even if the airplanes are going to London or Paris.

Angela smiled as she thought about her middle child. Susannah had a bit of a lisp in her elementary days. One day she came home and told Charles that there were twiplets in her class. Turned out to be true. The triplets belonged to a very high executive of one of Hexi-All's major competitors. Parents' night rolled around, and Charles went to Susannah's class. There, indeed, was Mr. Big sitting in a seat designed for a nine-year old. Mr. Big was not designed for that size seat, but, for that matter, neither was Charles. Both were enduring the evening and actually enjoying it.

Then along came Andrew. Andrew was born in 2026, twelve years ago. Margaret was a freshman in New Canaan High School by then, and Susannah was approaching twelve. Andrew might not have been planned, but he has been a major blessing to everyone in the family. Charles, then well into his forties, was very pleased to have a son.

Andrew adopted the New Canaan ways early on. He wanted to go away to prep school even before he started Kindergarten. Angela believes that Andrew will go into medicine. "He loves math and science and has sincere empathy for one and all. It's way too early to tell, but those early traits are important," Angela is quick to add.

Things were rocking along very smoothly for the Henderson family until about two years ago. That's when Charles was offered the job of a lifetime. The President of Hexi-All called Charles into his office and told him he had an opportunity he wanted Charles to seriously consider. The unofficial corporate translation of that sentence is: "I have an offer for you that you really should take."

An opportunity can be very, very good or it can be another word for pure Hell. The company President said that he wanted to take Charles out of the law department and give him a major job in operations. Now, those who know the energy business know that an executive in an operational job usually makes more money and can go higher on the career ladder that a staff executive.

Charles and Angela talked and talked and talked. Angela said she didn't want to stand in Charles' way of advancement. Charles said he would be away a lot more and have heavier burdens, which he wanted to be sure Angela understood Angela finally said, "Go for it!"

Charles told the company President that he would take the job. It turned out that the job was President of the company's Libyan affiliate. The original plan was for

Charles to start as Vice-President and then move into the affiliate presidency after a couple of years.

But the President of the affiliate, Dilbert Smythe-Goettinger, who was British of course, got himself arrested on the orders of Colonel Moammar Hassan. The Colonel was a great-nephew of the former leader and was now holding the shaky role of Supreme Leader of Libya by the skin of his teeth.

Dilbert was unceremoniously kicked out of the country for making moonshine in his garage. The charges were clearly trumped up because Dilbert was a bit of a prude and would never have touched the stuff. The new Colonel just wanted to show everybody who was boss. The Colonel also wanted to deal with someone less experienced than the banished Brit. Enter Charles.

Charles' new professional life started on a miserable note. On Charles' first day, Colonel Hassan staged a fake rebellion and tried to blame it on Hexi-All. Charles lived near the Colonel. On his way to work, Charles was stopped by a nervous non-English speaking Sergeant. The Sergeant said something to Charles in Arabic and then held him at AK-47 gunpoint for ten terrifying minutes. Charles escaped when actual gunfire erupted down the street, and the Sergeant ran to see what was happening. After that incident, Charles got a Libyan driver and enrolled in an Arabic language course.

Things calmed a bit after that crisis. Charles held most of his important meetings in Rome to escape the wiretaps and bugs and other inconveniences. Hexi-All put a private plane at Charles' disposal; so he was not completely stuck in Libya's capital.

It also helped that Hexi-All discovered a massive oil field out in the Libyan Desert. All of a sudden, Charles became one of Colonel Hassan's very good friends.

But the Colonel had some real and serious enemies. It is said that in the Middle East, "An important man has few friends and many, many enemies." They also that "The enemy of my enemy is my friend." Not exactly.

Charles was preparing for his monthly visit to Rome when he received a six AM call from the company pilot. "Sorry, Boss," the pilot said, "But I can't get permission to take off. Seems like there's another crisis of some sort in the government Looks like you will have to go LOL" The ex-pats referred to Libyan Airlines as LOL or "Lots of Luck" airline and so started the worst day of Angela's life.

Libyan Airlines Flight 3406 from Tripoli to Rome took off at 0900 local time. It was scheduled to turn left off the runway, climb to 15,000 feet and make a 15 degree right turn and then make a beeline for Rome. Flight 3406 dropped off the radar at 0930 barely into the Mediterranean without any indication of trouble and was never heard from again.

There was no wreckage, no black [actually orange] box nor any other physical evidence of Flight 3406's ever having existed. It was one of the great aircraft mysteries of all time.

The Libyan government disclaimed any knowledge or fault in what happened, and that may well be true. But the tragedy lives on for 112 passengers and crew and their families and friends.

The tragedy lives on for Angela in a terrible way. She spent six weeks in Libya trying to find answers where there were only questions. The U.S. Embassy was sympathetic, but the officials had no idea why a well-functioning airplane went off the screen. Even the Libyan government adopted a somewhat sympathetic tone but was quick to note that far more Libyans than Americans were missing. Sabotage was a definite possibility; but where was the proof and by whom.

Angela did her best to keep up the morale of her family in this critical period. She believed with all her heart that Charles would have wanted her to carry on the family tradition of the annual Christmas gathering in New Canaan. She would just have to overcome her sense of longing and sorrow. After all, she and Charles lived a happy life and the good memories overwhelmed the few bad ones. True, this would be a tough time for her in many ways, but she told herself Charles would want her to share the peace and joy of the Advent with the children and grandchildren. She could do it; she would do it!

With that thought in mind, Angela felt more peaceful than she had in months. She thought she just might lie down on the daybed and get a few minutes rest before Margaret and her family arrived.

Gabriel, Angel's own private guardian angel, was watching all this from afar and he could take no more, For an Archangel, he had a very soft heart – at least where Angela was concerned. Angela was his favorite human, and he knew what he had to do.

Suddenly Angela's sunroom erupted in a blaze of light and Gabriel appeared in his standard white garment, "Gabriel," said Angela in astonishment. "Is it really you?"

"Yep, it's me," replied Gabriel.

"Angela," he said, "I am terribly sorry about Charles. I am forbidden to change human history, as you know. So I could not interfere with Charles' taking that plane, although I knew its fate. But I am not forbidden from telling you what happened; and that may help you some.

There was no sabotage—just a series of awful events. The plane went off course over the Mediterranean and collided with an unmarked plane full of insurgents intent on toppling Colonel Hassan.

The pilot of the rebel plane had no idea the commercial plane was near, and the commercial pilot had no idea the military plane was near. Nobody had the right radar going. The Libyan air controller left his station at a critical moment to go to the bathroom. There is no excuse for what happened. If it will help, I will tell you the Libyan government is about to secretly ask the U.S. Government for help in finding the plane. Charles' plane will be found early next year, but nothing will ever be said about the rebel plane or the AWOL air controller. Again, I am very sorry."

Gabriel continued. "Charles was warmly welcomed into God's presence. He was met with the assurance that he had a new home. God told Charles, "Well done, good and faithful servant. You have been a wonderful husband and father. Angela and all your children will miss you more than words can express. Take comfort in knowing that you will be together when the time is right." On a different note, I will tell you that God thinks Charles has a splendid baritone voice and we have already made a place for him in the heavenly chorus."

One more thing: You are right to carry on the family traditions as best you can. Charles would want you to do that, He would also want you to carry on with your life. Think of all the joy you have brought Charles and so many others. Some days will be painful for you, but God still has things for you to accomplish. Charles would want that, and you know what – I want that for you too. Goodbye for now, but I will be watching over you your entire life. God be with you little Angel.

Angela awoke from her nap happy that she had regained her composure. Her first surprise was when Susannah walked through the door, Angela couldn't believe her eyes.

Jean-Marque had insisted that Susannah join the Henderson family for their cherished tradition, even though he couldn't make the trip. Jean-Marque Du Ret moved a notch higher in Angela's son-in-law estimation for that simple act of kindness.

Then Andrew knocked on the door, He had gotten off a day early from boarding school so he could have an extra day with his family. In fact, the headmaster himself had driven Andrew down from Upper Connecticut.

Angela was almost speechless when she saw Dr. Thomas Goodson arrive with Andrew in tow.

Then the expected happened. Margaret and her family arrived from Washington, D.C. Angela could have sworn that the twin girls had grown several inches since she had last seen them. Angela tried to imagine that they looked just like Charles; but they didn't. They had golden tresses—just like Angela. Otherwise, the girls were the spitting image of their father. Fortunately, he was a good-looking man and thank heavens, they didn't have Charles' nose. Now that was not a nice thing to think. Angela laughed to herself. And you know what, in her mind Angela could hear Charles break out laughing as he agreed with her completely.

"Come in, come in!" Angela called out. "Merry Christmas, all you beautiful munchkins!"

After that Christmas, Angela's acute attacks of sadness lessened somewhat. She was more likely to have dreams or daydreams of pleasant memories or, as she called them, attacks of the reveries. Life does go forward, thought Angela, as she surfaced from one of her daily New Canaan naps; so will I. Gabriel sensed a major change in Angela at that point.

"I believe Angela has turned a corner," Gabriel said to himself. And Gabriel smiled, feeling better than he had in almost three earthly years.

CHAPTER 13

GABRIEL APPROVES
A SECOND TIME AROUND

It is Advent season of the year 2043, and Angela has decided to spend Christmas with her brother, Michael Trufelli, and sister-in-law, Jennifer in Angela's hometown of Abington, New York. Angela, healthy and active in her mid-fifties, has been a widow for some five years now. The pain of Charles' death has eased considerably, but it sometimes re-appears, triggered by a memory or even a chance occurrence.

Angela's remaining child at home, Andrew, is spending this Christmas in Estes Park, Colorado, with a prep school classmate. Angela encouraged him to do so, since Andrew would be starting college next year. "Better take it." Angela told him, "You may not get another invitation."

Neither of her other two children, Margaret or Susannah, could make the trip to Connecticut this Christmas.

Margaret was busy in Washington, DC, with her family and their own holiday traditions. Susannah had just given birth to her second child, Collin Philippe du Ret, in Paris. Susannah enjoys explaining to the French relatives where the name "Collin" comes from and to her American relatives how the name "Philippe" was chosen.

Angela decided to fly to Abington even though it is less than two hundred miles by road. However, some of the roads can be very treacherous in wintertime, particularly as you get closer to Abington. Angela went to LaGuardia via the always reliable A+ Limo Service. A+ was owned and operated by a retired New York police sergeant, Tony Lombardo. Tony had started his company ten years ago with a used Cadillac station wagon driven by him or his son, Pat. Now A+ was a genuine fleet of ten vehicles, with Tony retired in Florida and Pat running the business.

Angela was waiting in the LaGuardia departure lounge when she spotted a familiar face. She wasn't sure she knew the man, but she was certain that she had met him somewhere. The man walked over to her and said, "Hello, Angela, I'm Jake Cole." The man turned out to be John Jacob Cole, her sister-in-law's older brother. Stranger still, Jake was on his way to Abington to share Christmas with Jennifer. Neither Angela nor Jake knew about the other.

Angela and Jake had a mini reunion while waiting for the plane to depart for Abington. Angela and Charles had, of course, known Jake and his wife, Martha. Angela hadn't seen Jake in over fifteen years.

Jake and Martha had divorced several years ago; and Jake lived a comfortable but single life in Highland Park, Texas. So, not only did Angela and Jake have Jennifer in common, but Jake lived in the town next door to Angela's college. Now more than ever, she was looking forward to her holiday time with Michael and Jennifer. Angela barely noticed that Jake was considerably older than she; Angela was just looking forward to her Abington visit and hearing more about her old college community.

Jake and Angela exited the plane, picked up their baggage, and were met by Michael, Angela's older brother. Michael was so glad to see Angela that he talked non-stop all the way to his house. Jennifer, toward whom Angela had experienced some slight teen-age resentment, greeted them at the front door like they had just been rescued from the jungle. As in the past, Angela quickly got over her prickly feelings about Jennifer and joined in the spirit of things. She was really glad to see both her brother and his wife.

Michael had been a tower of strength for Angela at Charles' funeral and afterwards. Charles had been Michael's best friend long before Angela decided Charles was the man for her. A person outside the family would have had a hard time deciding who was the more broken up by that fateful plane crash—Angela or Michael.

Michael also stepped in and did his best to comfort his nieces and nephew. Angela would never forget her brother's loving kindness.

The holiday season of 2043 went very well for those gathered at the Trufelli family's home in Abington. Michael and Jennifer were wonderful hosts to Angela and Jake. Many old friends came by to visit with Angela and Jake, but there were two sets of visitors. Jake's friends were much older than Angela's friends, but that didn't seem to matter. All got along well.

On the day Angela was to return to Connecticut, Jake asked Angela if he could come see her. He thought it might be fun to take in a New York restaurant and show. Angela readily agreed. Jake said, "Okay, how about right after the first of the year." That worked for Angela, and she agreed. They exchanged e-mail addresses and telephone numbers and went their separate ways.

Andrew, when he found out about all this, couldn't help teasing his mother about her new boyfriend. When Andrew had suggested something like this before, he had earned a playful cuff to the back of his head. Angela had no interest in re-entering the dating game. This time, Angela just blushed. "Uh, oh," thought Andrew, "maybe I am on to something."

Jake and Angela had a great time in New York. They ate in Little Italy at a restaurant where they hauled you in off the street, telling you they had the best pasta this side of Sicily. Jake, showing a sense of humor somewhat like Charles, said, "You know, I think they just made us an offer we can't refuse." The food was great, as advertised.

They went to see the show, but both were a little overstuffed with linguini and clams and the rest of a full meal. Jake observed that the restaurant had served real clams, not some sort of clam paste. They would return to Salvatore's Ristorante on many occasions thereafter.

Both Jake and Angela said that they should take things slowly under the circumstances. She had enjoyed a happy marriage with a bad ending, and he had endured a sad marriage with the right ending. They both had children. His were well into middle age, and hers were still relatively young, particularly Andrew.

Jake was never one to procrastinate though. He decided Angela was the one for him. He didn't want to waste whatever time he had left. Jake very much hoped for a second chance at marriage, this time with Angela. Jake was quite well off, even after the divorce. He would have no problem supporting Angela, although she could certainly support herself in good style.

Jake decided to pop the question on Valentine's Day. They agreed to a Valentine's Day date in New York. They would dine at Salvatore's and go see the latest musical on Broadway.

Jake flew up with a diamond engagement ring that would have been the envy of Elizabeth Taylor. He got so many Neiman-Marcus InCircle Points, the new president of the store, Stanley Rothschild, personally delivered the ring to Jake.

At Salvatore's, conspiratorial waiters arranged for a four-piece string ensemble to play tableside while Jake got down on one knee and proposed. Jake later told Angela that getting down on one knee was the hardest part of the proposal. He was deathly afraid that he would tip over the table and spill a very good bottle of red all over Angela. Jake offered Angela the ring, which one envious female bystander labeled the Rock of Gibraltar.

Angela was more than a little surprised by Jake's athletic proposal as well as by the size of the ring. This did not seem to her to be taking things easy. She was on the verge of telling Jake that she thought they should wait awhile longer, when the woman at a nearby table offered up that if Angela didn't want this guy, she would definitely take him. That was too much for Angela.

Actually, Angela had already decided to marry Jake. He just didn't know it. She did, however, want to put it off a bit. Then the thought struck her. "This is really stupid, Angela. Jake is 74 and you are 54. What are you waiting for?" She was ready for her second time around. She imagined that she heard her friend Gabriel herald his beautiful trumpet, at that very moment. Imagination working overtime again, mused Angela.

So, Angela gave Jake her most dazzling smile and said loudly enough for all the nearby busybodies to hear: "Yes. Let's do get married!" Jake smiled and managed to get up; the waiters cheered; the woman at the next table, who turned out to be Salvatore's wife and amateur matchmaker, also cheered.

Angela and Jake never made the show. They had been adopted by the Italians. Italians are very fond of good food, but they are even more fond of *amore*. The newly engaged couple was trapped. Some of the customers started to sing a piece from an opera. Neither Angela nor Jake had any idea which opera or what the words meant. But they were pretty sure that the song was all about *amore*.

A large man, who looked a lot like an older Marlon Brando, appeared at tableside. He offered Angela and Jake his congratulations and said their sizable check was on him. Jake decided this was also one of those offers best not to refuse and responded with his very best *Grazie*.

Salvatore laughed and said, "Your heart is good, but your Italian is awful. Be our guest, tonight."

Angela and Jake decided to have a small family wedding in June of 2044 at a destination locale.

They chose Bermuda. Both had been there several times, and they loved the pink coraled beaches and laid-back way of life. They rented the Pink Beach complex in Tucker's Town. Jake and Angela had considered the Southampton Princess, but they felt that a more intimate resort would be better.

Their small wedding turned out to include 90 people. Dr. Ted Walther, Angela's pastor, and son of Bishop Bill Walther of the Missouri Conference performed the ceremony. It was a beautiful event. The numbers for bride's side and groom's side were almost even. Both Angela and Jake had a large family, plus there were some people they just had to invite.

Angela moved her things into Jake's Highland Park home without a moment's hesitation. He did have to do some re-modeling to change the atmosphere from bachelor quarters to family home. However, Jake kept his sacrosanct study just as it had been for the last ten years.

Angela wisely avoided that foreboding place of sheer masculinity. This amused Jake no end because his study had been designed by one of Dallas' foremost doyennes of good taste, and she was definitely feminine in appearance and taste.

Jake had been a world traveler in his younger days. He had been to six continents and would have gone to Antarctica had he not contracted malaria in Africa.

Angela, on the other hand, had been to very few of the bucket list places in the world.

Angela had gone with Charles to some of the European capitals and, of course, to a few places in Africa when Charles was assigned to Libya. Now that Andrew was headed for college in September, she felt free to travel wherever Jake wanted to go.

Their first excursion was a riverboat trip down the Rhine, and Jake wanted to start immediately. He signed them up for the only cruise available—Adventures on the Rhine. Unfortunately, the cruise sailed from Switzerland on November 6, a little late for the sunny season. Angela gamely went along with this plan, although she had been to Switzerland in early November and knew that it was raw, cold and often rainy. "What the heck? I'm a newlywed," she told herself.

Well, it was raw, cold and rainy. But Jake didn't seem to notice. His French and German were almost as good as his Italian, which made for an interesting voyage. Everyone on the boat spoke English; however, people out in the countryside spoke very little English. Or so they claimed. But the natives seemed to genuinely appreciate Jake's efforts at Deutsch or Français.

Jake frequently earned a smile from a pretty shop girl when he valiantly tried to set her at ease in the local language as he sought to buy Angela a Diet Coke or a caffè latte, called coffee with milk in Germany and café au lait in France.

However, his chivalry backfired in the French city of Colmar when he very modestly said in French that he didn't speak French and tried to buy two caffè lattes. The shop girl replied in a French easily understood by Jake that she agreed with Jake that he didn't speak French. Jake wasn't too terribly upset by this rejection—anyway she wasn't all that pretty.

Every stop along the Rhine produced a magnificent cathedral, many of medieval vintage. Some of the cathedrals took hundreds of years to finish. A few of the places on the Rhine dated back to the Roman Empire. Rome couldn't pacify the tribes on the east side of the Rhine; so it needed fortresses on the west bank to protect what Rome called Gaul.

Many of the castles along the Rhine were in ruins. It would appear that the Germans haven't forgiven the French for destroying some of their major castles in their many wars over the centuries. For Americans, it is hard to imagine a grudge lasting five hundred years. In Europe, that is no time at all.

Angela and Jake returned from their Rhine voyage and immediately signed up for another trip. This time, they would travel during a more hospitable time of the year. "How about Alaska," said Angela. "And let's go in July." Jake agreed, and they signed up for July 2045.

Cruise time rolled around; and Jake and Angela prepared for their second adventure. They decided that they would take some sort of trip every year until one of them grew tired of traveling or until one of them couldn't manage the trip.

They flew into Vancouver, BC, and boarded a luxury cruise ship sailing the Alaskan inside passage. The ship stopped at Sitka, Juneau, Skagway, and several other exotic northern points. They ended up in Seward and took a train to Anchorage. Then they departed on a bus for Denali National Park. Jake, despite his many travels, had never seen Mt. McKinley—or Denali as the locals called the mountain.

The first day, a guide took them out into the wilderness. Just as advertised, there were bears and eagles in abundance. Denali inspired awe in the Indian population long before the US acquired Alaska from Russia. It was a spiritual type of awe; and Jake and Angela felt it too. You had to be close to God in a setting like this.

Angela thought Jakes's and her travels were an important part of this great chapter in the early part of their new lives.

CHAPTER 14

GABRIEL'S GLORIOUS GARDEN

It is early December and a bit chilly in Highland Park, Texas. Nevertheless, Angela Trufelli Cole is luxuriating in her morning off from her usual church and volunteer responsibilities. Angela has been a resident of Highland Park for a little over a year and is knee-deep in local activities after the tragic death of her first husband, Charles Henderson and remarriage five years later to an older family friend, Jake Cole. She moved in with Jake, sharing his long-time family home in Texas. A few months ago, Angela felt a major fix-up-the-house urge. Jake gave her carte blanche to remodel the house to her taste. Angela hired a local decorating firm, *Rejebian Re-Dos*, to help her freshen up Jake's very nice home on Beverly Drive.

Kathy Rejebian, granddaughter of the founder of Rejebian Re-Dos, had exquisite taste but caused Angela some heartburn over the cost. Jake said not to worry about the cost: "Do it your way," he said; so she [or more accurately, they] did. Angela decided to defer to Kathy's thinking about the final touches to their home because Kathy's auto wasn't due back in Angela's driveway until another two weeks.

In the meantime, Angela decided to visit her new next-door neighbor, Laura Smith. Laura and her husband, Winston Spencer Smith, moved in about a month ago. There are unpacked boxes all over the place. Laura and Winston are in their mid-forties, and their only child, Lawrence, is attending University in Lugano, Switzerland. Angela and her first husband, Charles, attended a Hexi-All Corporation conference there about fifteen years ago. The setting was gorgeous. Their hotel room overlooked Lake Lugano, and Angela fantasized about staying there the rest of her life. Such a dream was totally unrealistic, of course, but that's what made it so much more fun.

There is a small park just off the main street of Lugano. The central attraction is a bust of George Washington. When Charles asked the concierge why the first George W. was there, that exemplar of crossed-keys dignity said he had no idea. But you don't challenge the Swiss, even the Italian-oriented ones. The next day the concierge cornered Charles and told him that the bust was sculpted in 1830, and that Washington was a local hero in the early nineteenth century. George Washington, of course, was never in Switzerland. He was a Virginian, although he marched all over the Atlantic seaboard fighting the redcoats and even had to live in New York as President while the Federal District was under construction. For that matter the father of our country only once ventured outside the territory that became the United States. He accompanied his brother, Lawrence, to Barbados for reasons of health—his brother's health.

"My, how I digress," mused Angela. "Back to the Reverend Doctor Smith and his lovely wife, Laura." Winston was the new rector of St. Michaels and All Angels Episcopal Church located on nearby Preston Road. He was properly called Father Smith or Father Winston, but he had insisted on informality when he first met his neighbors. The Smiths had recently moved from a smaller church in Longview, Texas, and were busily getting acquainted with their parishioners and their Methodist neighbors, as well. Highland Park is blessed with many, many Methodists, partly because of Southern Methodist University.

Angela was a little intimidated by Laura's credentials in the gardening department. Angela felt like she had only a pale-green thumb when it came to such things as aromatic herbs, various variegated shrubs, oz-hued zoysia lawns, tall trees, and various other items in the vegetable kingdom.

Laura, on the other hand, was a certified Master Gardener. She had trained at the feet of a fellow minister's wife in her old neighborhood in the pine hills of East Texas. Laura's Longview neighborhood bore the charming name of Robinwood Acres. What's more Laura had recruited Winston into that rare fraternity of Master Gardeners.

Of course, there aren't many pine trees in Highland Park, and what few there are in the DFW Metroplex are rather puny compared with the acid-soiled giants of East Texas. Laura had, for some reason, named her Longview garden Gabriel's Glorious Garden. There in the center of her garden was a "life-sized" statue of the Archangel Gabriel. (More about that later.)

Laura had already visited Galloway Farms, a noted Dallas-area tree nursery. She decided to con–

centrate on plantings that were native to the area. Laura found two varieties of maple trees that do well in the Dallas area and hoped to plant a sapling of each variety in her yard. Yards are somewhat smaller in Highland Park compared with many in other parts of Texas and certainly compared with those in the affluent parts of the Eastern United States, where two, three, five-acre and even larger lots are common. Property values in Highland Park might be a factor and could certainly cause one to think that the Highland Park soil was composed of 18 Karat gold rather than dirt.

Angela wasn't sure what it took to be a Master Gardener, so she researched in the place everyone else does in this era: *Wikipedia*. She found that the Texas Master Gardener program is decades old and is conducted by the Texas Agri-Life Extension Service of the Texas A&M University system.

Master Gardeners are members of the local community who take an active interest in their lawns, trees, shrubs, flowers, and gardens. They are required to have special training in horticulture through their county's Texas Agri-Life extension office to provide horticulture-related information to their communities.

But that is just the tip of the iceberg. If accepted into the program, a volunteer is required to attend over 50 hours in specialized training courses. Then the Master Gardener-to-be must do volunteer work in the county office and elsewhere. Participants become certified Master Gardeners after they have completed the training course and fulfilled their volunteer commitment. The program is for serious gardeners only.

Okay, mused Angela, I think I will just stick with my Church and other volunteer work and let Laura be the Certified Master Gardener. But Angela was more than a little curious about Laura's story of the life-sized statue of Gabriel in the midst of Laura's former Longview horticultural paradise.

Watching this from his heavenly perch, the real Gabriel chuckled at his favorite human's curiosity. He could sense human thoughts. Deciding it had been far too long since he had seen his Angela, Gabriel donned an appropriate disguise and took a small journey to Earth.

"Good morning," Gabriel cheerfully greeted Angela at the side entrance to Father Smith's backyard. Angela was a bit surprised to see the bearded man in old fashioned overalls and pushing a wheelbarrow containing some sort of object covered in burlap. "My name is Carlos Angelo," the man said, "and I got a call from the Church to help Father Smith's wife with the heavy loading part of her backyard refurbishing."

Angela replied, "Laura will be back soon, and I am sure she will appreciate your help."

Angela's curiosity got the better of her at this point. "What's in the bag?" she blurted.

"Oh, it's a statue of the Angel Gabriel," replied the incognito Gabriel. "Mrs. Smith had one in Longview and asked the church to try to obtain one in the Metroplex. We found a wonderful copy just before the Smiths arrived."

"Mrs. Smith offered to reimburse the church for the expense, of course, but I don't think the vestry will allow that. Senior Warden Holman Prince wouldn't hear of it."

"Here, look at this masterpiece," enthused Gabriel, as he uncovered the seven-foot statue. "Gabriel is my favorite Archangel," the gardener bragged.

"Well, actually he is my favorite angel, as well," replied Angela and Gabriel nearly choked up on that unexpected response. Gabriel wasn't supposed to be emotional about humans, but he made an exception for Angela.

Laura returned about that time and had a brief conversation with the gardener. The gardener progressed to the appropriate spot in the backyard and began his work.

Laura had just intercepted the mail carrier and was leafing through the day's mail. She apologized to Angela telling her that she and her husband were expecting a letter from their son, Lawrence, who was attending a wonderful university in Switzerland. Lawrence was going to spend his winter/Christmas vacation in Paris and she and Winston were almost as excited as Lawrence about that. But no letter was in the mail. Angela told Laura not to be worried; young people these days use nearly every other form of communication medium before even thinking about using the postal facilities.

Laura Smith's prayers were not to be answered in the U.S. mail. She learned her son's whereabouts, not from him, but from the nightly news. A group of terrorists had targeted the *Café du Montmartre* district of Paris' *Rive Gauche* and were holding over 200 hostages at that moment. There had been some gunfire earlier in the evening, but things were calm on the exterior at present. It was a little after 10:00 PM in Highland Park but Paris was seven hours later. The television scene was a true nightmare. Ambulances were screaming at the TV audience and the entire setting was worse than any horror show. The news media were playing the worst scenes over and over.

American and French politicians and other talking heads were occupying the little screen panels and generally making matters worse, particularly for the families of the hostages. It took the Smiths awhile to register that Lawrence might be in the midst of the action. In one sense, not knowing was as bad as confirmation, thought Laura. Laura Smith then picked up her cellphone and called the person she felt most comfortable with in her new location – her next-door neighbor, Angela.

Trying to absorb the new crisis, Angela threw on some clothes and rushed next door. As she expected, the Smiths were in a total state of anxiety. They knew their son was in Paris, but they didn't know where. For the first time in her life, Laura wished Lawrence were a girl. Girls tell you where they are going [at least some do, some of the time]; young men would die first. Oh, what an awful thought that was, Laura told herself.

Then the call came. Laura's cellphone rang. It was Lawrence.

He was hiding in a storage room in the basement of the café. Fortunately, there was a tiny window – open, but entirely too small for an escape. But he was sure the terrorists, or whoever they were, would come looking for him and anyone else who had fled the immediate scene. Lawrence reminded himself that they were masked, which was good. That meant there might be survivors. Maybe they were just after money, and not bent on killing for the sake of revenge or some other sick idea. He had hope.

Then the line went dead, and Lawrence was gone to Laura. No, Laura thought, this is worse than not knowing. He must have been discovered, I must go to him at once, Laura decided.

Laura turned to Winston and said, "I am leaving for Paris just as soon as I can pack and get a plane ticket." Angela, a bit impulsively added, "And I am going with you." Winston was a bit nonplussed that he had obviously been left out of the rescue, but he knew that neither his doctor nor the airline would let him fly this soon after his eye surgery.

AA 48 cleared runway 35L at 7:28 PM, headed nonstop for Paris' Charles de Gaulle Airport. Laura and Angela were occupying seats 3H and 3J in the business section. Father Winston and Angela's husband insisted that, under the circumstance, Laura and Angela should take the more comfortable section of the plane and forego the hassle of economy class travel.

Before leaving, Angela asked a favor of her first husband's employer, Hexi-All Corporation. The corporate security chief of that giant conglomerate said a car and driver would meet Angela and Laura at the airport and take them to the Georges V Hotel. After a short rest, they would be briefed by one of the corporation's security agents. Hexi-All's foreign security information rivaled that of the State Department in some areas of the world.

That afternoon, Angela and Laura met with Andre Lecarre, Hexi-All's security manager for France. Andre told them that the situation was in a quiet stand-off phase between the terrorists, if indeed that was what they were, and the French authorities. One problem was that the French authorities were still smarting over the last incident and were inclined to send in the Charles de Gaulle Gendarmée National and just storm the place. Andre said the terrorist leader was a Swiss national with a Middle East background. He called himself *Le Chacal*. Furthermore, his home region was Lugano in the Italian Swiss area.

Andre agreed to introduce Angela and Laura the following morning to the head of the Gendarmée National, General LeClerq. Angela decided that was a great idea, for she thought that she and Charles Henderson had met the great man at a conference in Paris a few years earlier. The meeting was set up for 10:00 AM the next day.

In his most Gallic manner, General LeClerq introduced himself to the ladies and greeted Andre as an old friend. For indeed LeClerq and Andre went back a long way and had shared some interesting adventures.

Angela, in her most charming manner opened with "*En-chantée, Mon General, mais je ne parle pas Français*," or in her best Texas English: I don't speak French. The General immediately was charmed and moved to English. This in itself was a huge compliment to Angela. But then LeClerq, being Parisian, didn't think a Burgundian like Andre spoke French either.

Angela addressed the General then in her most charming English: "General, I wonder if you might consider a different approach with the terrorists. I hear that their leader is from Lugano, with an origin in the French speaking portions of either the Middle East or Northern Africa. Laura's son, Lawrence, whom we believe to be in the hands of the terrorists, is currently living in Lugano. Perhaps he could be helpful to your negotiations."

The General was intrigued by the idea. Actually, the French Premier wanted no more bloodshed; and the authorities weren't even sure the captors were true terrorists, even though there had been some gunfire early in the assault. The ambulances were just a precaution and actually no one had been reported killed or wounded. LeClerq then said, "I will have our negotiator call the terrorist leader and suggest that Mrs. Smith's son and the leader talk thing over calmly. "Excellent idea, General," responded Angela, dodging who really conceived the strategy.

Le Chacal reacted positively to the negotiator's suggestion and called for Lawrence Smith to come forth. Lawrence approached the leader and the leader did an instant double take. Le Chacal, in fact, was Lawrences' landlord in Lugano, Lawrence had no idea of the identity of the masked terrorist. To protect his identity Le Chacal called one of his men over and told him to tell the young American that they were going to release him with instructions for the French authorities. The Frenchman told Lawrence that Lawrence was to take the following demands to LeClerq:

> We want the immediate release from jail of two of our men – Jean Montecristo and Louis Dreyfus, and you must arrange their prompt transfer to the Café du Monde.

> We want a fully fueled and ready-to-fly 15 passenger helicopter on the rooftop of the Café by Midnight. We have our own pilot.

> Your understanding that we will take two hostages with us to a destination in the Middle East where we will release them unharmed and leave your helicopter, and

> Oh, by the way, we want 5 million Novo-Euros, the new European currency.

Le Chacal told the Police negotiator that he would have no more use for the hostage Lawrence Smith, so there was no need for him to return to the café.

Angela and Laura Smith were thrilled beyond measure to see Lawrence when he arrived in General Leclerq's headquarters. Lawrence passed on Le Chacal's demands and then added a surprise of his own. "General, I know who Le Chacal is. He never spoke to me; however I recognized his slight but unusual limp when he walked away from me. He's my Lugano landlord, Phillipe

Cluseau. He was born in Tunisia, but he has extensive holdings in Switzerland., including a large villa near Zurich. I heard him talking with one of his employees about renting a helicopter to travel between Lugano and the Zurich airport. I would bet a month's tuition that he plans to take your helicopter to the Zurich Airport and ditch it there."

"I gather you think I should comply with his demands," said a slightly irritated LeClerq.

"That's up to you," said Lawrence, "but my captors looked to me like a thoroughly trained and prepared combat team," said the young man.

Angela, ever the charming and somewhat sly fox, added, "General, you would be a national hero if you rescued the hostages and then captured the villains, even in another country. Why don't I go as one of the hostages," volunteered the brave Angela. "A thousand times no, dear lady,' said LeClerq. "But one of the hostages in the café is a part of my secret service and she will take the place that you have so valiantly volunteered to occupy. Your service to France will not go unnoticed, our brave Madame Angela. And it is not true that you do not speak French. Your French is *magnifique*."

And so Lawrence was rescued and Angela's trap was set.

As Lawrence, Laura and Angela were departing Charles de Gaulle Airport on AA 49, Nonstop to DFW Airport, General LeClerq and a team of Swiss and French commandos eagerly awaited Le Chacal's helicopter in

Zurich. The Swiss are very methodical, and sure enough, Le Chacal's flight landed in Zurich exactly as expected.

The two hostages were freed, but only after the undercover agent planted a serious knee blow to Le Chacal's middle body region when he tried to grab her and escape. All the criminals were placed in Swiss custody, awaiting extradition to an angry French nation. The 5 million novo-Euros were counterfeit, so they didn't matter very much. But the Swiss gave the French their helicopter back immediately, as a token of good international relations.

Just before his Christmas homily on Christmas Sunday, Father Smith asked Angela to give a brief account of her adventures in Paris and then to read St. Luke's New Testament account of the birth of Jesus. Angela gave her best two-minute summary of Lawrence's rescue and then opened her King James Version of the Bible to Chapter 2 of The Gospel According to Luke.

As Angela finished the reading and returned to her seat, the bearded gardener left his seat in the back pew and quietly departed the church. One parishioner heard the bearded stranger say, as he left, "Amen, and well done, my lovely Angela."

And Gabriel smiled.

CHAPTER 15

GABRIEL VISITS HIGHLAND PARK

It is late November in the year 2047 and Angela Trufelli Cole is enjoying a rare mid-afternoon treat in her "new" hometown of Highland Park, Texas. How anyone could re-create a vision of the high mountain area of Colorado in the recently expanded Highland Park Village [a pioneer Texas upscale shopping center] was beyond even Angela's very active imagination. But someone did, and Angela was luxuriating in the local version of an Aspen spa. "New" might not be exactly the right word for Angela's re-location to Texas. While living in the Northeast, she had been a supportive alumna of Southern Methodist University, her college home located not far from her present residence.

Nor was Angela exactly a newlywed, either. She was three years into her marriage to Jake Cole following the tragic death of the first love of her life, Charles Henderson, in a middle eastern plane crash. Angela had been enjoying a great life in New Canaan, Connecticut (the next stop to heaven, according to local lore) when life dealt her a crushing blow.

Angela was far more the type to count her blessings than to brood over her losses. She felt very blessed by the joys that **life** had afforded her so far, namely two great husbands, three wonderful children, and some perfect little members of the third generation. In Angela's view, **life** was to be lived perhaps coincidentally Angela and Jake's favorite play is *Fiddler on the Roof*; and Angela loves the musical tribute to *L'chaim* – **To Life**. "If our good fortune never comes, here's to whatever comes – *L'chaim, L'chaim, L'chaim,* **To Life!**"

Angela brands Tevye, the milkman and star of the show, as a truly great philosopher. The scene that brings tears to Jake's eyes, however, is when Tevye sees one of his daughters off to Siberia at a remote Russian railroad flag-stop to follow the daughter's dream – and her love [never fails to bring tears to the author's eyes, either; guess we never let them go.]

[But returning to our story;] While neither Jake nor Angela is a born Texan, Jake brags that he got to Texas as fast as humanly possible. Jake adopted his new hometown of Highland Park in his twenties upon gradu- ating from nearby SMU.

Jake's actual hometown is Abington, New York, a beautiful spot in Upper New York State, nestled in the hills, and sporting a very cold climate. Angela, along with her first husband, Charles, shared that New York hometown with Jake; and Jake had been a friend of An- gela's family for years. Angela didn't know Jake well when she was young because of their age difference. But that point didn't seem to matter to Angela now. Once An- gela makes up her mind, she never entertains second thoughts.

"It was love at second sight," she mused, thinking about her whirlwind romance with Jake starting four years ago. However, I fully realize that there is a third "person" in my life, Angela reminded herself. "I have a guardian angel who has looked out for me since I was very young." Yes, Angela is the beloved friend of the Archangel, Gabriel, and Gabriel takes very special care of her. Gabriel approved fully of, even encouraged, her marriage to Charles, then he gave his sincere blessings and encouraged her second time around with Jake.

"Enough of this spa-inspired daydreaming," thought Angela as she snuggled into a gigantic towel and breathed in the soothing aromas of the spa. "I just love the Scandinavian life," mused Angela. I should have been a Viking." Gabriel occasionally tuned in to Angela's thoughts from afar, as he sat on his heavenly perch; and his reaction was: "I don't think you are cut out for the raiding life my dear Angela.

Gabriel himself led a busy life as God's spectral special messenger but he always found time to care for his favorite human, occasionally stretching his instructions and helping matters along – always in the right direction, of course. Angela had no idea that Gabriel sometimes discerned her thoughts; but it really wasn't like he was snooping. After all, Gabriel was God's right-hand angel and assigned to look out for her.

Returning home from the spa, Angela was warmly welcomed by Jake and their newly arrived houseguests from Washington, DC, Bill and Melanie Bates. After a few minutes, the Bates excused themselves to prepare for Angela's evening event. But Melanie returned shortly and knocked on Angela's door. Melanie told Angela how pleased she was to see Angela leading such a happy life with Melanie's old friend, Jake. Angela told Melanie that she and Jake loved every minute of their time together. Melanie asked Angela if she would be offended by a personal question.

"Absolutely not," Angela assured Melanie, "and I am pretty sure you are going to ask me if other people have a problem with Jake's and my age difference."

"Yes," said Melanie. Bill is older than I am, fabulously wealthy and always in the public eye. I find that tough sometimes."

Angela replied, "I do understand what you are saying, but Jake and I just go on with life; and very importantly (to us, anyway), our families and most of our friends have been completely supportive. On one of our trips, no one on the boat, except the couple traveling with us, even suspected that Jake was 77 and that I had clocked almost 57 years myself.

"We are planning the trip of my dreams next Spring – a small private group tour of a dozen or so exotic spots in a modified Boeing 757 – very roomy seating, no check-in lines, and no security hassles. Plus, the plane just goes directly from one wonderful place to the next. It's almost like traveling in a huge private plane, something you and Bill can do anytime you want to."

[As an aside Dear readers, Jake had known Melanie years ago when she was single and living in Texas, and they shared a deep friendship. Melanie later transferred to Washington to work with her television network. While there, she met and married Bill Bates, a multi-billionaire media mogul. Bill's business thrived and now they are both multi-billionaires "God bless Washington," said Melanie on numerous occasions.]

But back to our story: Melanie had returned to her room to continue dressing for the gala and Angela was thinking about her dream trip. Yes, sometimes Angela was bothered by spending such serious money on herself when there was so much poverty in the world, even in her surrounding area but, Jake wanted to take this trip while he still had the energy, and Angela wanted to please Jake.

Anyway, Angela thought it would be romantic to visit the Taj Mahal, and perhaps some of the other wonders of the world, as well. Angela and Jake could afford the trip. She had been left well off when Charles died; and Jake had been quite successful in life – in spite of a very expensive divorce years ago,

"Okay, enough of this," thought Angela. "I have to finish getting ready for the big annual fund-raising dinner for a great charity, "The Holiday Gala for United We Stand." "Holiday G-U-S was the short-hand way Angela put it. With Angela's hard work, imagination, and charm, the Gala had quickly evolved into a major Dallas event.

Last year the Gala had netted more than a million dollars to support local education for children from impoverished neighborhoods. Angela had always been drawn toward helping children and this project had been greatly enhanced by putting Angela, with her energy and determination, on the board; and then this year, the Board asked Angele to chair the Gala. Jake took a backseat role but he was supportive, as always. Jake had grown up in a modest, middle-income household, similar to, but with somewhat more long green than Angela's own family. Angela and Jake weren't even close to the Bates' financial condition, but they certainly didn't have to worry about paying for the next latte.

When Angela finished dressing, she joined Jake in his study. He gave her some really worrisome hot-off-the-press news. There were unofficial reports from Asia about a viral breakout in an isolated Chinese village. The World Health Organization said local health authorities had determined that the situation was under control.

"But," said Jake, "who knows what that really means?" And what made the current story even more worrisome was that the events reported happened over a month ago.

Angela thought uneasily back to the time of another such incident, not all that long ago. The distressing news of 2019 was about a coronavirus outbreak in Wuhan, China. That situation was downplayed by a number of governments, including the United States government. Americans were told they had nothing to fear; the new virus was a Chinese problem.

Angela had a Texas cousin, a Dallas lawyer, about to meet his niece in London in late February 2020 on an extended weekend. They had plans to take the usual sights in and around London. Fortified with good news from his government, Angela's cousin didn't worry much about a Chinese coronavirus.

Sure enough, it turned out that the cousin (and his niece) didn't catch even so much as a sniffle, while British princes were coming down with Covid-19 and the UK Prime Minister almost died from the disease, the tourist from Texas did suffer a final indignity of enduring a 10 hour flight home with the occupant of the seat directly behind him coughing harshly with every other breath. Angela's cousin was one lucky tourist; or maybe Gabriel was protecting him as an unsolicited favor to Angela.

[Now back to the future.] The Gala was scheduled to begin at 7:00 PM. Angela was expected in the Green Room at 6:00 PM, exactly one hour prior to H-hour. But at 5:30, just as our team was about to leave for the hall, Angela received a text asking her to make an urgent call to Henry Brown, the General Manager of the Event Hall. Angela went back inside the house and placed the call. Mr. Brown, clearly beside himself, told Angela that the Gala was off.

The County Health Department had just delivered an emergency health lock-down order Furthermore a few minutes ago the President had declared a State of Emergency that covered the entire states of California and Texas. The CDC called the new culprit Covid-47; and a Covid-47 outbreak in Houston had already hospitalized over 300 very sick people. Initial reports said that Covid-47 was worse than Covid-19 or any variant thereof. Apparently, the Houston victims had been exposed to a super-spreader who had recently deplaned a Dallas to Houston flight, as continuing travel from Shanghai to Los Angeles to Dallas.

Angela was heartbroken thinking of all the disappointed gala-goers and the children and schools that would be affected by the loss of the failed fundraiser; but she fully supported good health and safety procedures. At roughly that point Jake and the Bates left the warm car and rejoined Angela in the house.

It was Angela's sad duty to give them the bad news. After the shock wore off somewhat, Melanie hugged Angela and declared, "Not to worry. Bill and I will fund the entire loss. We can't restore the lost evening with all its fun, excitement, energy, and inspiration; but we won't let your kids down." Angela was for one of the few times in her life, completely speechless- for a moment anyway. "Thank you so much, Melanie – and Bill. I guess I have two guardian angels – besides Gabriel, of course." Melanie Bates had no idea what Angela was talking about; but she recognized 100% pure selfless gratitude when she saw it.

Then, with her kids cared for and her Gala team notified, it dawned on Angela that her own dream trip was fading fast, at least insofar as the near term was concerned. No way would she and Jake be going to all those wonderful places next spring. Angela went back to her room to have a good cry.

That was too much for Gabriel. He went to the man with the kind face and applied for an immediate leave to go visit Angela in person to comfort her once again. Leave granted. In the blink of an eye, a blinding light appeared at Angela's bedside white she was now fitfully dozing after such an emotional episode. "Uh, who's that? Jake?" asked the partially awake Angela.

"No, it's just me," replied the grammatically challenged Archangel, brilliantly attired in his white robe.

"Gabriel, I am so glad to see you," enthused the now wide-awake Angela. "I am just crushed by the awful news that our world is threatened once more, and so soon after the great pandemic. We lost so much back in 2020-2021. Yes, I am grateful that so many did survive to get back up and continue with life. But it was rough."

"That was indeed a hard time for humanity," agreed Gabriel. "At the worst, people lost loved ones, friends, family, leaders, not to mention confidence, jobs, income, nest eggs, and sometimes their very lives It was a bad time, and yet, the human will to survive, to love, to comfort, and, as you would say, to stay in the game, prevailed."

Angela asked at the point "Do you think we can do it again?"

"Oh, yes. Without a doubt," responded her guardian angel. "just as the dawn of 2022 foretold the dawn of the post-Covid-19 era, Covid-47 will be subdued by science and sound leadership – sooner, I think, than the great pandemic."

"Serious as Covidi-47 is to those affected, it can be stopped much quicker this time. The science of messenger RNA vaccines is much more advanced today, and just as important, most countries don't have a bunch of crazies in charge of the circus. There is no real conflict between science and religion except as schemes put forth by people with a selfish interest in creating conflict. I know that's tough talk coming from an Archangel—but you, Angela, have never blinked from the truth, when you figured it out."

"Wow!" responded Angela, "Am I actually hearing what I just heard from God's right-hand messenger?"

"Yep," replied Gabriel, "your Abraham Lincoln was right. You really can fool some of the people all of the time – at least for a while. But I have noticed that throughout history you Americans have tended to learn from your mistakes, and at some point cease to be fooled."

Gabriel added, "I have to go now, but I leave it to you as to what you do with the knowledge I have just passed on. You can be a prophet, if you choose; but beware, prophets not only tend not to be honored on their own turf but are prone to be attacked without reason or mercy. By the way, there will be a Holiday G-U-S next year, but it will be called the "Bates-Cole Gala" because of an endowment Bill and Melanie Bates will bestow on the "GUS" in your honor. Nice people. Got anything you want to add before I go?"

"Well, yes Gabriel, I do," said Angela. I appreciate you more than I can ever express. I am not at all sure that I am cut out to be a prophet, not that I fear the truth or the consequences of telling the truth – when I know what the truth is. You have given me much to think about. Thank you. Thank you so much. You are very much my favorite Archangel," added Angela. (Gabriel exited with, "Must get back to my duties. God bless you, Angela.")

About that moment, Jake entered the room, and Angela asked him if he had seen an archangel sur–

rounded by a blinding light. "Afraid not. But are you okay?" asked an anxious Jake.

"Never been better. But I feel really sorry for my friends who have missed a really good Gala this year. But I know that next year will be much better," said Angela. Jake smiled, admiring how resilient Angela was. She never let the winds of fate beat her down. Angela would be there for her kids and for all her benevolent interests for the rest of her long life. What a woman, thought Jake; I am so lucky.

Two weeks passed with Covid-47 seemingly under control as Christmas neared. The Pastor of Angela's church asked Angela to come down to the church to help him with an important project. He wanted Angela to participate in a Christmas video to be shown to the thousands of online streaming viewers who participated in HPUMC services and other programs via virtual media.

On the scheduled day, Angela was asked to read the Christmas story from a text of her choice. She opened a KJV Bible to the Gospel according to Luke, took off her mask, faced the camera and started reading.

Luke, Chapter 2:

"And it came to pass in those days, that there went out a decree from Caesar Augustus that all the world should be taxed."

Angela finished the reading and took a seat in the third-row pew. She felt a strange mixture of warmth, humility, pride, gratitude, and awe.

Meanwhile, Gabriel was engaged in an animated discussion with the man with the kind face who told Gabriel that Angela had read the story of his Bethlehem birth very well. "Yes," replied Gabriel, "I believe Angela fully understands the true meaning of Christmas." Thinking of Angela always made Gabriel smile; and he did so at just that moment. Then the man with the kind face added, "By the way, that was quite a conversation Angela had with my favorite archangel a fortnight ago." Gabriel reacted to that award with an even wider smile. As a human might say, Gabriel grinned from ear to ear.

CHAPTER 16

JAKE "INVADES" RUSSIA

Angela lost count of how many cruises, trips, and adventures she and Jake enjoyed during their life in Highland Park. She remembers that they traveled to every continent. Jake was glad to re-live his travels and was delighted that he finally got to see Antarctica.

They did have one close call. They were on an extended cruise in international waters near the northwestern territory of Russia when Jake felt a sharp pain in his lower right abdomen. Jake had suffered a minor bout of possible but undetermined appendicitis in his twenties; but the doctor didn't think surgery was required. Jake felt that the problem this time was serious.

The ship was small, and Angela feared the medic aboard was barely qualified to remove an infected splinter, much less an inflamed appendix. The ship had Norwegian registry, and the captain wasn't about to make an unplanned entry into Russian waters. The captain agreed to return to Norwegian territory and put Jake off at a port near a regional hospital about ten degrees below the Arctic Circle.

Angela was not very happy about this development. They had more than enough trip insurance to cover a medical evacuation. She wanted a jet plane to Dallas or New York—and right now. However, by the time they got Jake ashore, there was no time left. The appendix had to go—STAT, as the doctors say.

The Norwegian hospital turned out to be a very good one. Jake said goodbye to his appendix, and they decided to hire a helicopter to rejoin the ship in St. Petersburg. It took some real diplomacy to get the Russians to allow a US – registered helicopter to land on their soil on such short notice. But one of Jake's friends in Washington talked his Russian counterpart into doing just that. Later, Angela and Jake joked about their detour and the American invasion of Russia and continued their world travels.

Angela and Jake had a good life. Both thoroughly enjoyed living in Highland Park. Angela got re-acquainted with Highland Park United Methodist Church, where she had been so involved in her college days. Jake was also an alum of SMU, and they had a great time getting seriously re-acquainted with their alma mater.

Angela was a docent at the George W. Bush Presidential Library. She loved to repeat, off campus of course, the tales that one of her cousins from Texas told her about how that prize almost escaped SMU because of a few weird preachers. The tales were fun but came from a lawyer and were no doubt exaggerated.

How could anyone doubt that a Presidential Library would greatly benefit a university? It didn't really matter whether you liked a particular president or agreed with his policies.

Angela simply could not understand this kind of destructive behavior on the part of otherwise intelligent people—at least some of them were intelligent; and some were otherwise, according to the cousin.

Her cousin told her that some of the most "otherwise" were a gaggle of bishops, many surprisingly from the heartland of America. Her cousin was eager to share his views on the subject: some Bishops deserve great respect as the royalty of the church. (No longer just "princes," except in a couple of faith traditions.) But some, blessed with a surfeit of pomposity and pretention, reveled in their episcopal persona, and a few, he felt, were as dumb as doorknobs.

Angela's cousin also admitted, rather guiltily, that some of the bishops were actually both wise and humble. He readily acknowledged his prejudices on the subject; for his father, a Methodist Protestant minister, had never forgiven his church for agreeing to an episcopacy in the long-ago 1939 merger. Big mistake, he thought.

Angela's family and its extensions grew over time, with children, grandchildren, and great-grandchildren. Her great-grandchildren were in northern Virginia and Florida; and she and Jake visited them as often as possible.

Jake liked the Sarasota weather in wintertime and would occasionally hint to Angela that they should move there. Angela didn't take that suggestion seriously for one minute. Jake was a dyed-in-the-wool Highland Park denizen and would always be so. Anything north of the Red and east of the Sabine was foreign territory and should require a passport to get in or out.

Jake developed a serious illness as he neared his 92nd birthday, and Angela worried that he would not make the century mark that they both confidently predicted he would reach. Jake, however, would remind Angela that he was a tough old bird. And he was.

Gabriel noted on his earthly calendar that Jake's time was nearing, and he feared that Angela would be in pain once more.

In February of his 94th year, Jake went to meet his Maker, as peacefully as a good night's sleep. Jake had been a good man and a wonderful husband to Angela. That was enough for Gabriel. Gabriel would personally go to earth and escort Jake to his heavenly home.

Jake's service at Highland Park UMC was upbeat and uplifting. The church had enjoyed a succession of able ministers whose very calling was preaching funerals and comforting the bereaved. The Rev. Arville Campbell-McDonald handled both roles very well.

Jake was indeed met by Gabriel and escorted to the man with the kind face. "You are welcome here," the man with the kind face said, "Gabriel will take good care of you. Do not worry about Angela, Gabriel will do that for you. He just cannot help himself. Come, you have some old friends here who would like to see you."

Gabriel could not help worrying about Angela. Gabriel looked down and saw that she was surrounded by dozens of family and friends. She was smiling and bragging about what a great husband Jake had been. Angela was once again very much at home as the loving comforter. Gabriel relaxed and once more smiled at the thought of his lovely Angela.

CHAPTER 17:

GABRIEL'S BUS

Angela (Trufelli) Henderson Cole was lying comfortably on her day bed in the sunroom of her beautiful home in Estes Park, Colorado. Snow was gently falling. It reminded her of goose down erupting from a shattered pillow after a pillow fight gone seriously wrong. What a silly thought! Angela mused.

Because of the clouds, she could not see Long's Peak in the distance, she felt a warm sense of security just knowing it was there. It was always there standing watch over the valley. Angela had lived much of her life in the East—in Abington, New York, and then in Connecticut. After her second husband Jake (a fellow New Yorker but adopted Texan) died, she moved from Texas to Colorado to be near her youngest child, Andrew Henderson, and his wife, Virginia.

And best of all—her twin grandchildren, Billy and Bobby Henderson. The twins had arrived late in Angela's life and were joy personified. They were eleven now and excited with the glow of Christmastime.

Angela had celebrated her 80th birthday the past August with a rip-roaring Colorado mountain party thrown by Andrew and Virginia, the local grandkids, Angela's two daughters from Florida and all their families and a few extra local cowboys and cowgirls—forty people. Angela thought it was amazing that she even knew 40 people, much less was a close relative to most of them.

They had celebrated out of doors—typical of western life. They then went on a hike around Bear Lake in Rocky Mountain National Park. The mountains towering over the lake are majestic, but the hiking trail around Bear Lake is almost flat—so much the better Angela had thought at the time. Angela didn't recover as quickly from exertion as she had when a mere 75.

As Angela thumbed through her Advent draft, she was quickly enveloped in a reflective mood. As she sipped a little sherry and munched on some of her favorite goodies, she felt she had much to be grateful for—loving children and grandchildren, two wonderful men in her life (both passed on now), a host of friends over the years, and a physical setting for her winter years of life that could only have been orchestrated by God. As an aside, she thought the twins looked a lot like Charles Henderson, her first love and the father of her three children—Margaret, Susannah, and Andrew.

Not that she hadn't dearly loved her second husband, but she would always miss Charles. A plane crash had taken him in his mid-fifties, and Angela still struggled with the seeming unfairness that transpires in the lives of God's children.

Then in her mid-fifties, some five years after Charles died, she re-discovered Jake Cole. Jake had been divorced for several years and had never considered another marriage until chance threw him in Angela's path. Jake was the older brother of Angela's sister-in-law Jennifer (Cole) Trufelli. He was visiting Michael and Jennifer in Abington during Christmas. As chance would have it, so was Angela. Things started slowly with them, particularly with the significant age difference; but matters heated up around Valentine's Day. They got married that June and had a wonderful life in Highland Park, Texas until Jake's heart gave out a few weeks before their twentieth anniversary. Jake lived well into his nineties but didn't make the century mark that Angela had so wished for him. To sum up her mindset, Angela didn't feel sorry for herself, she just felt that she had been doubly blessed.

Now, however, her own fortunes had taken a turn for the worse. Her son Andrew was a great doctor and could easily have had a Park Avenue practice. Angela was extremely proud of Andrew. His grades had always been outstanding, and he graduated from Harvard College and Harvard Medical School with an equally splendid record. The New Canaan public school system was among the very best, public, or private, in New England.

Andrew wasn't interested in big city practice. He marched to a different drumbeat. He married a 21st century version of a mountain woman and moved to Estes Park.

There Andrew set many broken bones and occasionally had to treat the reckless and foolish who braved the east front of Long's Peak—under-skilled or underdressed. Twice, he lost patients to that unforgiving mountain. Andrew's inspiration for medical practice had been the legendary Dr. Pierre Schlesinger, who more than once saved Angela's life.

Andrew had called in several specialists to confer about Angela's condition; but they were in complete agreement – in every day "Angela language," absent a change in scenery (altitude too high, weather too severe), she was living on borrowed time. My, I'm rambling, thought Angela.

With such thinking and maybe a little extra sherry, Angela drifted off into a dreamy trance and thought back to a time more than 70 years ago—to the time of her greatest theatrical triumph and the first time she met the Angel Gabriel.

Angela greatly enjoyed her memories of meeting Gabriel and his help in her first starring role in the church Christmas pageant—how strange she thought there I was being coached in my role by the very character I was to play. Gabriel.

❄ ❄ Suddenly Angela awoke with a start! ❄ ❄

Standing there in the room beside Angela was the most gleaming figure she had ever seen—in life or dream. "Gabriel," Angela said; "is that you? I haven't seen you in a hundred years," Angela exaggerated, "but I would know you anywhere."

"Yes, it's me," replied Gabriel "and actually, it's been thirty of your years since we last talked."

"I am so glad you're here," Angela exclaimed.

"I came in my bus," responded Gabriel.

"You did what!" replied a confused Angela.

"Look, out on the street; there's my bus. I don't just act as a messenger or musician. Sometimes I take very special friends for a ride on my bus. Want to come along?"

Angela had always been bright, and she got the message immediately. "Is it my time for the bus ride?" asked Angela.

"I'm not quite convinced," replied Gabriel. "What do you think? You have a host of friends waiting to see you. You have made many people happy over the years. The Chief smiled all day long when I told him I had your ticket."

"Can I say goodbye to Billy and Bobby?" asked Angela, as she took the ticket from Gabriel's outstretched hand.

"I am afraid not," responded Gabriel, "but I promise you they will understand."

"I'm prepared for the bus ride but not quite sure the grandchildren are ready," said Angela.

Gabriel looked pensive for a moment, then nodded in understanding. He held up his hand and said, "You're right. Besides, there is something that I need to do before we leave. Let me have your ticket back, please."

The snow had stopped falling, and just as quickly a bright sun lit up the afternoon sky. The grandchildren came into Angela's sunroom a few minutes later with their mother. The children told Virginia that they had heard their grandmother talking with someone.

"Can't be," said Virginia, "There's no one in here but your grandmother, and she must be sleeping, look at the smile on her face."

"I wonder where she got that piece of shiny white cloth she is holding in her hand?" asked Billy.

"I have no idea, "replied his mother," But let's just let her rest awhile.

"Good idea," said Billy; "she seems so happy; we can see her later."

Billy and Bobby started back toward the kitchen, but there standing in the living room was a man dressed in the whitest suit they had ever seen. "I know you," said Bobby, "You were the trumpet player in the band at Nana's 80th birthday party last summer."

"Yes," said the man, "My name is Gabe, and I am an old friend of your grandmother, although I don't think that she recognized me at the party. I first met her when she played the Advent angel in a Christmas pageant long ago. She was the best Advent angel there ever was. You do know what Advent means, I suppose?"

"Sure," popped off Bobby, the more assertive twin, "it is about preparing for the coming of the Christ Child."

"Right," said Gabe.

"To change the subject a little, I know that you went to see the re-make of the old movie, The Lion King, last month, right?"

"Yes, it was great," said an impressed Bobby.

Gabe then said, "Doesn't happen often, but that movie got it exactly right. Life really is a circle and even though your grandmother is very sick, she will live on forever because she has you and her other grandchildren. I must go now; actually, I have to catch a bus."

"By the way, you may not know it, but your grand-mother really has a guardian angel, and if you ever need help, I am sure her guardian angel will come looking for you in a nanosecond," said Gabriel, inordinately proud of his high-tech vocabulary. Then, he just vanished into thin air—at least according to the story told by both twins.

"Wow!" exclaimed Bobby, after Gabe left, "What do you think of that dude?" "Dressed all in white, framed by the picture windows, with the sun beaming in on him, you might mistake him for an angel."

"Can't be," said Billy, "He was a guy and didn't even have wings. Even though he looked much younger, he must have been an old friend of Nana's. Pretty smart, though, for a trumpet player."

"Hey, hold on," said Bobby, the trumpet player in the family.

"What do you make of the strange conversation?" Bobby asked Billy.

"I would say, it sounded just like Nana," replied Billy. "She has always been my guardian angel."

"Yeah, mine too." said Bobby.

"Let's go see if Nana's all right," added Billy.

Rushing into the sunroom, they were surprised to see Angela wide-awake and staring out the window to-ward the empty street. "Nana," said Billy, "we just met a friend of yours—all dressed in white and talking sort of weird."

"Yes," replied Angela, "that would be Gabriel. He's been my friend for many Advents."

"Is he a good trumpet player?" asked Bobby.

"Oh, yes," replied Angela, "the best. But I learned today, for the first time, that he also drives a bus."

"Are you going somewhere with him, Nana?" Asked Billy.

"Yes, but not today," replied Angela. "Perhaps the next time Gabriel comes for me in his bus, I will take a ride with him. Today, however, I must finish my Advent story for my Sunday School Class, the Wonderful Wesleyans. It's all about the coming of the Christ Child. And I also want to tell my two little munchkins what Christmas means to me." said Angela, with a twinkle in her blue eyes that would match any of the stars in Gabriel's realm.

Angela's grandchildren shrugged at being called munchkins, which they thought might be something like Christmas elves. But they knew that munchkins must be lovable little people because Nana only used that name with her grandchildren and then only shortly before she grabbed and hugged them. Which is exactly what happened next.

Angela had faced some difficulty writing her story this year because her class had suffered through a bout of influenza. Nearly a dozen members had contracted the disease, and some had serious aftereffects and the class had lost two members. Angela had a hard time writing upbeat prose when her friends were hurting so much; but she carried on and did her best.

Over time she herself had lost two beloved husbands, other family members and close friends. Angela remained very grateful for all God had given her. She believed with all her heart what the pastor had said in a recent sermon – worry won't add a minute to your life, and it can rob you of some of your time and most certainly can rob you of peace and joy.

Angela penned a thankful prayer to her Advent story as she wrote "The End" to the last of her long line of Advent stories, about 25 she figured. Yes, she would end her last Advent story on a joyful note. Glory to God in the highest, and on Earth, peace, and joy to all.

Meanwhile, Gabriel's bus rounded the final turn of his journey and stopped at the front door. "Everyone out," ordered Gabriel, "We're here."

"Welcome," said the man with the kind face. Privately he turned to Gabriel and asked, "Are you one passenger short?"

"No, it wasn't Angela's time," was the reply. "Perhaps she will take the bus on my next trip," Gabriel added. The man with the kind face pondered Gabriel's answer a minute and then said, "You're right. After all these years, Angela is still making Advent come alive for all my children, young and old. Of course, there will always be a place for her in this house. Well done, once again, wise, and faithful messenger."

And once more, Gabriel smiled.

CHAPTER 18

ANGELA TAKES A RIDE
WITH GABRIEL

Our setting for this chapter is the year 2070 and this story coves the years 2070-2076. Angela turned 81 in August of 2070 just two months before moving from Estes Park, Colorado, to Sarasota, Florida.

Last year, Angela survived almost having a bus ride with the angels in Estes Park, Colorado. The Archangel Gabriel decided that it wasn't her time to board the mysterious bus. The children and grandchildren could have some more time with their beloved Angela.

Andrew Henderson was Angela's youngest child, only son, and the father of Angela's beloved twin grandchildren, Billy, and Bobby Henderson. Andrew was a renowned orthopedic surgeon who moved in the mid-fifties from the East to Estes Park to escape the crowds, as he put it. The spring after Angela almost died, Andrew sadly told his mother that her health required a warmer climate. Andrew, in fact, was afraid that Angela might not make it through another winter as severe as the winter of 2069-2070.

Angela, no stranger to relocating, decided to move in October of 2070 to Sarasota, Florida, to be near her other children—daughters Margaret and Susannah. Susannah and her husband Jean-Marque du Ret had moved from France to Sarasota in 2050 and loved the area, as did their children—Charles Auguste (now 30) and Collin

Philippe (now 27). Both of Susannah's children are lawyers specializing in estate planning. There is a huge market for such services in Sarasota.

Margaret and her husband Patrick Beall retired to
the area about five years ago in 2065. The Beall children,
twin daughters Marie and Grace, live in the Washington
DC area with their families.

Both Margaret and Susannah live on Siesta Key
and love the calm, the climate, and the culture of the area.

So, in the fall of 2070, Angela moved again—this
time to Siesta Key in Sarasota County, Florida. In the mid-
twentieth century, Siesta Key was a sleepy island in Sarasota County, just off the mainland. It hasn't been sleepy
in several decades. In the mid-twenty-first century, there
are numerous fine homes and a number of midrise co-
ops right on the beach.

Angela chose a two-bedroom co-op on the fifth
floor of one of the midrises. Her building enjoyed private
beach privileges to some of the most beautiful white sand
on earth. Angela quickly regained her health and was
soon in the thick of things.

Angela joined the Sarasota Yacht Club, although
she vowed she would never buy a boat much less a yacht.
But she did enjoy going out into the Gulf on Susannah and
Jean-Marque's boat. Angela joined a golf club and was an-
noyed with herself that she could no longer golf her age.
Angela decided that she was acting a lot like Daisy, the C.
C. Young resident of her college years.

Angela's charm and personality soon won her a
suitor at the Yacht Club. The female to male ratio of

essentially healthy seniors in that part of Florida is about 5 to 1; but Angela wasn't very interested. She had enjoyed two wonderful marriages and decided to opt out of a third. Her suitor was ardent, though. He wasn't just an ordinary well-to-do retiree. Dr. Rudy Mayo had been Chief of Surgery at Johns Hopkins, and there was still plenty of fire in the old fellow's soul. He had clear blue eyes just like Angela's first love, Charles Henderson.

He also had an unusual physical trait for a man in his 80s—a full head of snow-white hair. Had he let it grow long, he could certainly have subbed for a skinny Santa Claus.

While marriage was only in one party's mind, Angela did like to go out with Dr. Rudy, as she called him. He was intelligent, enjoyed a fair round of golf, and played a near perfect hand of bridge. He was very good company. Before long it was apparent to the friends of both, that Rudy was **taken**—just not legally.

Angela's daughters were a little worried that Dr. Rudy might be one of those Florida fortune hunters because Angela had been well provided for by both husbands. "Nonsense," Angela told them. "I might be after his money, though" she joked. "Didn't you catch that he is a doctor and that his last name is Mayo? Besides, Rudy and I aren't going to get married. I have had two great husbands, and I am not going to break in a third, regardless of how attractive a prospective groom he may be."

Rudy and Angela joined the Siesta Key Community Chapel in 2072 and became very active members. Angela specialized in senior citizens ministries now rather than in children's programs. To be candid, she sometimes felt a yearning in her heart for those years when she directed children's pageants or youth programs. Time marches on, she mused, a little sadly.

Angela had a nasty fall near her 83rd birthday, and she and Rudy decided that it was time to take their ages seriously. With the help of her daughters, they found a retirement complex called Bay Village, located just south of Sarasota off highway 41.

Bay Village started as a Presbyterian establishment but was a stand-alone facility now. It was a living arrangement for seniors at all three levels.

You could have an apartment for independent living, but with meal privileges, if you wanted them; you could have some assistance in your arrangements, if you so desired; or you could have hospital like care. Many seniors just moved in and stayed for the rest of their lives. That is what Rudy did a year before Angela bought her space in 2073, when she was 84.

Angela recovered from her fall and happily moved into Bay Village. Rudy met her on arrival. Their apartments were just down the hall from each other. They took their lunches in the complex dining room but usually had dinner together in one of their apartments. Sometimes they ate out at a local restaurant. Rudy guarded his driving privileges as though his life was at stake. He was actually a pretty good driver—all things considered.

They gave up golf but continued their yacht club membership for another year. Rudy was undoubtedly the best bridge player Angela had ever met. They formed a Bay Village Bridge Club, and Rudy and Angela never came in below second—usually first.

Their close friends, General Sir Alastair Macbeth and his lovely wife, Lady Pamela, were frequently their bridge table opponents. Both were excellent players. Sir Alastair was a retired general of the British commandos. He didn't talk much about his Army experiences, but he amused Angela no end because he often addressed Rudy as "old thing"—as in, how are you, old thing?

Rudy passed first. He developed melanoma the second year he was at Bay Village. Due to his medical skills, he knew just what his problem was and how serious. Recent medical advances in the field helped Rudy outlast almost everybody who had ever had the aggressive form he developed. Nevertheless, at 85, Angela laid to rest her third special companion. The chapel service was beautiful and recognized the spirit and accomplishments of a truly great man.

Everything has its season, thought Angela. I too have lived a long and fruitful life. I have been blessed in many ways and count myself as the luckiest woman who ever lived. She caught what she had just said, chuckled to herself, and silently apologized to Lou Gehrig for borrowing his famous words.

The Archangel Gabriel watched these events unfold from his heavenly perch. Angela was his favorite human, and whatever moved Angela moved him. A tear formed in the Archangel's eye as he thought about Angela and her special life. He was there to help her when she was eight and he was there to help her when she was eighty. Gabriel knew that Angela was near the end of her time. She had had a close call six years ago in Estes Park, and her time was approaching. "Of course," he said to himself, "all earthly things must end at some point."

It is almost Christmas day, 2076, and Angela, now 87, isn't feeling well. She has mustered enough energy to have a Christmas surge with Billy and Bobby Henderson, her eighteen-year-old twin grandsons. They arrived fairly late in her life and are now freshmen at Southern Methodist University, Angela's alma mater. Billy and Bobby elected to spend this Christmas with their much-loved grandmother in Sarasota. Angela enlisted them to tell the Christmas Story to the residents of Bay Village. The twins are happy to do whatever they can to please Angela because they consider her their guardian angel.

On Christmas Eve, the twins read the Christmas Story from Luke to the assembled seniors, and you could have heard a pin drop when the ancient story was read by the twins.

The Gospel according to Luke
Chapter 2

And it came to pass in those days, that there went out a decree from Caesar Augustus, that all the world should be taxed.

2. (And this taxing was first made when Cyrenius was Governor of Syria.)

3. And all went to be taxed, everyone into his own city.

4. And Joseph also went up from Galilee, out of the city of Nazareth, into Judea, unto the city of David, which is called Bethlehem; (because he was of the house and lineage of David)

5. To be taxed with Mary his espoused wife, being great with child.

6. And so it was, that, while they were there, the days were accomplished that she should be delivered.

7. And she brought forth her firstborn son, and wrapped him in swaddling clothes, and laid him in a manger, because there was no room for them in the inn.

8. And there were in the same country shepherds abiding in the field, keeping watch over their flock by night.

9. And, lo, the angel of the Lord came upon them, and the glory of the Lord shone round about them: and they were sore afraid.

10. And the angel said unto them, fear not, for, behold, I bring you good tidings of great joy, which shall be to all people.

11. For unto you is born this day in the city of David, a Savior, which is Christ the Lord.

12. And this shall be a sign unto you; ye shall find the babe wrapped in swaddling clothes, lying in a manger.

13. And suddenly there was with the angel a multitude of the heavenly host praising God, and saying,

14. Glory to God in the highest, and on earth peace, good will toward men.

15. And it came to pass, as the angels were gone away from them into heaven, the shepherds said one to another, let us now go even unto Bethlehem, and see this thing which is come to pass, which the Lord hath made known unto us.

16. And they came with haste, and found Mary, and Joseph, and the babe lying in a manger.

17. And when they had seen it, they made known abroad the saying which was told them concerning this child.

18. And all they that heard it wondered at those things which were told them by the shepherds.

19. But Mary kept all these things and pondered them in her heart.

20. And the shepherds returned, glorifying and praising God for all the things that they had heard and seen, as it was told unto them.

The residents were fascinated. Angela, of course, beamed her approval at her awesome offspring. She just loved the King James Version of the Christmas story. It was a glorious Christmas day and she felt much better in her heart.

Gabriel drove up in his bus on the day after Christmas. Gabriel felt in his heart that this time Angela would know her time had come to board the bus. Gabriel stopped off at the guesthouse where the twins were staying to greet them before he picked up Angela. Gabriel, now in his gleaming white attire, asked the boys if they remembered him.

They did, and they asked him if he was there to take their grandmother for a ride on his bus. "Yes," Gabriel answered, "it's time."

Billy said at that point, "We understand what you mean, but we can barely stand the thought of Nana taking that ride."

"I have much the same feelings, myself," responded Gabriel.

Gabriel arrived at Angela's co-op and woke Angela from a sound sleep. She looked at him and recognized him instantly. "Hello, my favorite angel," said Angela.

"And hello to you, my favorite human," responded the Archangel.

"Is it time for me to take a ride on your bus, Gabriel?"

"Yes," said Gabriel, "Here's your special ticket." Angela took the ticket, got up, and to Gabriel's amusement, went into the next room to put on her best dress.

Gabriel went out to the bus and waited for Angela. When she appeared, he took her ticket. The bus started off slowly but rapidly gained acceleration.

At their destination, Gabriel got out of the bus and joined a nearby group. Then Angela was greeted with the magnificent strains of a beautiful choral piece—something akin to the Hallelujah Chorus. The Archangel Gabriel was leading the chorus, playing his trumpet—the best Angela had ever heard. Gabriel asked Angela later if she thought he was in good tune. "Better even than at my wedding," she responded.

Gabriel showed some more very un-angelic behavior by tearing up again, and Angela was quick to comfort her very favorite angel with her own loving spirit.

During her welcome, Angela looked at the assembled chorus and spotted her mother, her father, Charles, Jake, Rudy, and some other familiar faces. And there, too, were her older brother and his wife—Michael and Jennifer. Then it was Angela's turn for a good cry.

"Come now," said the man with the kind face, "No need for tears. Here you will find eternal peace. My grace may have enabled you to get here, but it was your own loving spirit and kind actions that earned you so many loved ones."

God stepped over to Angela and gave her a big hug, repeating what he had told Charles 38 earthly years ago: "Well done, good and faithful servant." Then just to her, he added quietly, "Welcome home, my lovely angel." Angela responded with her most winning smile.

And once more, the Archangel showed his approval of his beloved, and indeed his very favorite, human.

And Gabriel smiled.

The End

www.ingramcontent.com/pod-product-compliance
Lightning Source LLC
Chambersburg PA
CBHW070925250626
47159CB00009B/3128